Alison and Jamie started to walk back to their soundstage through a deserted part of the lot, where old, massive props sat like dinosaurs in the sun. Suddenly, Alison grabbed Jamie's arm.

Jamie stared at her. "What is it?"

"I just got the weirdest feeling. Like someone was following us." She turned and glanced over her shoulder. The sidewalk was empty.

"Hey, are you letting that crazy fan letter freak you out?"

"I . . . maybe I am," Alison admitted.

"Look, if you're safe anywhere, you're safe here," Jamie said. "Anyway, there's no one following us. Look for yourself."

"You're right." Alison laughed shakily. "I'm just being silly, I guess."

Trouble in Paradise

ILENE COOPER

PUFFIN BOOKS

PUFFIN BOOKS
Published by the Penguin Group
Penguin Books USA Inc., 375 Hudson Street, New York, New York 10014, U.S.A.
Penguin Books Ltd, 27 Wrights Lane, London W8 5TZ, England
Penguin Books Australia Ltd, Ringwood, Victoria, Australia
Penguin Books Canada Ltd, 10 Alcorn Avenue, Toronto, Ontario, Canada M4V 3B2
Penguin Books (N.Z.) Ltd, 182–190 Wairau Road, Auckland 10, New Zealand

Penguin Books Ltd, Registered Offices: Harmondsworth, Middlesex, England

First published in the United States of America by Puffin Books,
a division of Penguin Books USA Inc., 1993

1 3 5 7 9 10 8 6 4 2

Library of Congress Catalog Card Number: 92-42427
ISBN 0-14-036158-8
Printed in the United States of America

High-Flyer™ is a trademark of Puffin Books, a division of Penguin Books USA Inc.

Trouble in Paradise

Chapter 1

Jamie O'Leary looked up and down the street. Why wasn't the studio limo here yet? she wondered impatiently.

Then she had to laugh at herself. A few months ago, she would have been waiting for a bus, not a limo. And her street would have been littered with garbage instead of sporting neat lawns and palm trees. Who cared if the car was a little late? She was now a star on a hit television show, *Sticks and Stones.* She should be thanking her lucky stars, not grousing about a late limo. "Watch it, girl. You're going Hollywood," Jamie murmured to herself.

"Talking to yourself now?"

Jamie whirled around. "You scared me, David."

David Gamble held up his hands in a gesture of apology. "Sorry."

"I'm sorry, too, David," Jamie said. She gave him a quick kiss on the cheek. "You just can't be too careful these days."

"You've spent too much time in New York."

New York. Just the words brought a little smile to her lips. Jamie and some of her co-stars on *Sticks and Stones* had recently come back from a publicity trip to the Big Apple. There had been a modeling assignment and lots of interviews, but the jewel in the crown was being a presenter on the American Choice Awards. Dressed to the nines, Jamie had mingled with the likes of Phil Donahue and Julia Roberts, and had appeared to millions of viewers around the world. It was probably the most exciting moment of her life.

"Earth to Jamie," David called.

Jamie focused back in on David. With his tousled blond hair and sky-blue eyes, he was easy to look at. Her heart fluttered. There was a lot to like about David and she did. Too bad he was sometimes an utter pain in the neck. David was an actor, too, but one who turned up his nose at television. His idea of acting was taking roles in dinky little plays in basements that no one ever came to see. She hadn't spent much time with David, just enough to know that he considered television beneath him. That really bugged her. If only he weren't so cute.

"You're back at home now, not waving to the *paparazzi.*"

Jamie wasn't a redhead for nothing. Sometimes her temper sparked like a flame. "I'm not some airhead starlet," she snapped.

"No, you a were child star on *The Happydale Girls,* and now you're a situation-comedy success on *Sticks and Stones.* A long, distinguished career."

"Listen, buddy, in case you've forgotten, there were long, hard years between those two shows. The only thing between me and disaster was my mother's job as a waitress. So, excuse me if I think being back on television—on a hit show, no less—is just a little bit of heaven."

David looked contrite. "Hey, I was only kidding around."

"No, you weren't. You think television is stupid. You've told me so a million times."

"I've only known you a couple of weeks," David protested.

"Yeah, a million times in a couple of weeks. That's what makes it so annoying."

"I helped you study your script a couple of nights ago."

Jamie snorted. "Yeah, and the whole time you kept reading lines in a fake British accent."

"Well, I had to give the thing a little class." David said the words innocently, but a sly smile played around his lips.

"I'm going to wait for the car in the house." Jamie whirled away from him.

"Hey, can't you take a little teasing?" David said as he grabbed for her arm.

His touch was enough to calm her down. She had never met a guy who evoked so many different emotions in her. "I guess I can," she finally said.

"That's good." He released her arm, but continued to stroke it lightly.

"Want to go inside?" she asked. "I think I'll have a cup of coffee while I'm waiting for the car."

"I can't. I've got to get to the cleaners," David said regretfully. "I've got an audition myself this morning."

"For something good?" she asked.

"A play out in the Valley. Wish me luck?"

"I do," Jamie said sincerely.

She walked back to the attractive duplex she shared with her mother and little sister, Elsie. David certainly could get her juices going. Sometimes she liked sparring with him, but he could go too far.

Or maybe it was just her. Jamie knew that she had been losing her temper an awful lot lately. A nagging little voice whispered to her, *It's because of that diet you're on.*

Oh no, it's not, Jamie protested to herself. The diet was doing just what it was supposed to, knocking off the weight and making her look great in clothes. The diet had started when Jamie became jealous of her co-star's model-thin figure. Not that Jamie didn't have plenty of other reasons to be jealous of Alison Blake. Alison was rich, had supportive parents, and, maybe most annoying, she hadn't even originally wanted the job on *Sticks and Stones.* She had just been attending the audition with a friend when she had been picked out in the waiting room by the show's producer, Dan Greenspan.

Even though she and Alison were finally on better footing, Alison had been a thorn in Jamie's side for a long time. Although also a redhead, Alison was the sweet, angelic type. "Lithe and lissome," the reviews of the show had called her. Jamie, on the other hand, had been described as having more "bounce to the ounce." Not that Jamie was fat. Curvy, was more like it. In fact, she had the kind of figure that drew whistles from most guys. But Jamie knew that the television cameras could make you look ten pounds heavier. That, and the fact that Jamie didn't want Alison to be the only one with a model's figure, pushed Jamie onto a stringent diet.

For a while it been difficult to diet, but Jamie found that it was getting easier all the time. Now, instead of counting calories, as she had at the beginning of her diet, Jamie just ate as little as possible. She had actually gotten to the point where she found food pretty repulsive. Jamie considered this a good sign. The more turned off by food she was, the less she'd be tempted to eat.

There was a downside, though. Jamie knew she was more snappish than usual. Only yesterday, she had yelled at her sister for putting on some of her lipstick.

Jamie felt embarrassment wash over her. She adored Elsie, and only a few months ago she would have giggled with delight to see her plain little sister with a big, red, lopsided bow painted on her lips. Instead, she had railed at Elsie about using her things, sending Elsie off to her room in tears.

If Elsie was awake, she'd make it up to her this morning, Jamie thought as she opened her front door. But the house was quiet. Jamie went over to the phone and saw the light blinking on the message machine. She played it back. The limo driver had a flat and would be there as soon as possible.

Well, that gave her few minutes. Jamie thought she

might have another cup of coffee—it seemed like she lived on coffee these days—but instead, she went over to the window and peeked outside. She half hoped David had decided to come back and join her, but the street was empty.

Oh, who cares? she thought grumpily.

"Is the car late?" Mrs. O'Leary came out of the bedroom, stifling a yawn.

Jamie looked at her mother in her new bathrobe, not that old ratty one she used to wear. One of the great things about being back on television was being able to buy her mother some of things she deserved. When times where tough, her mother had kept things together. Now, it was Jamie's turn to make things easier for the family.

"Yeah. He'll be here soon. But you don't have to be up this early," Jamie said. "Now that you've finally quit your job at the Tick Tock, you can sleep as late as you want."

A worried look crossed Mrs. O'Leary's face. "I'm not sure I made the right decision."

"Why not? Now you get to stay home with Elsie, just like you've always wanted to do."

"I know, that's the nice part." Mrs. O'Leary sat down on the couch. "But I don't feel right having you be the sole support of this family. Why, you're not even sixteen."

Jamie shrugged. "Now that the show is a hit and we know it's going to be on for a while, there's no point in you wearing yourself out serving up slop to a bunch of tourists."

"Jamie," Mrs. O'Leary protested, "the Tick Tock is a very classy place."

"If it's so classy, why didn't they ever pay you a decent salary?"

"I made pretty good tips," her mother said softly, looking down at the floor.

Boy, Jamie thought, her mother and Elsie were two of a kind. Just look at them funny and they felt terrible. "I know you did," Jamie said wearily.

"Well," Mrs. O'Leary said, brightening a little, "at least we'll be getting some money from your dad."

Jamie couldn't hear mention of her father without having her stomach tighten a little. Jack O'Leary had been her manager when she was on *The Happydale Girls,* but when the show disappeared, he had, too. Her mother always tried to make excuses for her husband, telling Jamie how hard it was for him, losing his job along with Jamie and not being able to find anything else he could make a go of.

He had come back periodically. During one of those visits, her mother became pregnant with Elsie, but that hadn't stopped him from going off again. Then, when he'd learned about Jamie's job on *Sticks and Stones,* he had reappeared, full of regrets and promises for the future. Jamie hadn't been fooled. She knew her father thought he could somehow creep back into her career, and she had put her foot down. But it had taken Alison to talk to him and make him see that he was hurting Jamie's career, not helping it. Mr. O'Leary had apologized to Jamie and told her things would be different, that he would get a job on his own. Jamie was taking a wait-and-see attitude. She knew her mother wanted them to be all together, to be a happy family, but even her dad had finally realized that wouldn't happen until he was able to stand on his own two feet.

"Has Dad gotten a job yet?" she asked carefully.

"No. But he's had a couple of interviews."

"Then the money won't be coming right away."

Mrs. O'Leary sighed. "I'm sure he'll get something soon."

"I hope so." She didn't dare say more. Any comments she could offer would only make her mother feel bad all over again.

"So how does it feel to be back at work?" Mrs. O'Leary asked, changing the subject.

"I guess I'm glad to be back. New York was terrific, but that was fairy-tale land. I want to get back to the old grindstone."

A blaring horn outside interrupted them.

"That's for me," Jamie said, grabbing her purse. "Have a nice day, Mom."

Once she was settled in the backseat, Jamie looked over her script. She was heavy into this week's show. The premise of *Sticks and Stones* was that a garage owner, Joe Stickley, had fallen in love with a wealthy divorcée, Amanda Stone. Jamie played Wendy Stone, Amanda's daughter. Rodney Janeway played her younger brother, also named Rodney, a little know-it-all, which wasn't that far off from the real Rodney's personality. Alison was one of the Stickley kids. She had an older brother, Lucas, played by the superattractive Mike Malone.

Mike. Jamie looked up from her script and thought about the brooding actor for a moment. When Jamie had first started on the show, she'd had her eye on Mike herself, but during the trip to New York, it had become pretty clear that Alison was the one who interested Mike. That figured. Alison had no problem getting everything she wanted.

By the time they pulled up to the soundstage where *Sticks and Stones* was shot, Jamie could feel a headache coming on. She didn't know if it was because she was hungry or just nervous about starting shooting again. What she had told her mother was true. She was happy about getting back to work, but it was nerve-racking, too. Despite all her years in the business, Jamie still worried that someday her talent would just evaporate. Poof! There she'd be, up on the stage, unable to utter a realistic word. She even had nightmares about just that scenario.

The soundstage was a bustle of activity by the time Jamie arrived on the set.

An assistant director came up to her. "The limo driver called us, but don't worry, you're not really late."

"That's good," Jamie said, relieved. Things usually started promptly on the set. "When will the reading start?" On Mondays, the cast sat around a large table and read over the script, seeing which lines worked. Informal and fun, Mondays were Jamie's favorite day.

The A.D. looked worried. "I'm not sure. Something weird is going on around here."

"Weird?" Jamie repeated, startled. Usually things were so professional on the set. Dan Greenspan ran a tight ship. It helped them all get a lot accomplished, which was a necessity when you were turning out a show a week. "What do you mean?"

He lowered his voice. "Dan was out of town for a few days while you guys were in New York. When he got back, he was giving out all sorts of weird vibes."

"And no one knows why?"

"Not even his secretary."

"Oh gosh, I hope the show's not getting canceled."

The A.D. shrugged. "Anyway, you have time for a cup of coffee and doughnuts, so go ahead."

Jamie looked with distaste at the breakfast buffet that was set up every morning. The last thing she wanted to do was fight off the urge to down a couple of doughnuts.

"Good morning, Jamie." Donna Wheeler, who played her mother, came up beside her. "You don't look like a very happy camper today."

"Just a headache," Jamie said, brushing aside Donna's concern. "Say, have you heard any rumors about Dan?"

"As a matter of fact, I have," Donna replied, lowering her voice. "Scuttlebutt says Dan's going to be making some big changes."

"In the cast?" Jamie asked with alarm.

Donna shrugged. "I'm not sure. But I understand he's going to be talking to us before we get down to business today."

Jamie's head started to pound with a little more vigor. She hated surprises.

A voice came over the loudspeaker. "Ladies and gentlemen, could you assemble onstage? Dan wants to have a word with us before we begin.''

''I told you,'' Donna murmured.

In groups of twos and threes the cast and crew moved toward the center of the stage. Jamie went over and stood beside Alison and Mike. ''I hope this isn't bad news,'' she fretted.

''I don't think it can be good,'' Mike responded. ''Dan's looking awfully grim.''

''Could we have been canceled?'' Alison asked. ''I thought the ratings were really good.''

''They are,'' Mike affirmed. ''We're a new show and in the top ten already. I don't think the network would want to get rid of us.''

''Then what? From the expression on Dan's face, it's got to be something major,'' Jamie said.

Mike shrugged. ''I think he's just about to clue us in.''

Dan stepped up to a podium one of the stage crew had placed in the middle of the stage. A boyish-looking man with frizzy hair and aviator glasses, Dan was usually full of smiles and good-natured jokes. Today, however, his smile seemed a little fixed, and he had to take several sips of water before starting.

''Well, gang, you're probably wondering why I've called you all together this morning. First of all, nobody's fired.''

A collective sigh of relief went around the room.

''But somebody is leaving. And that somebody is me.''

Now there was dismayed chatter, and Dan had to clap his hands to get everyone's attention back.

"To be honest, I'm not very happy about this. *Sticks and Stones* was Kate Morton's and my baby, and what a baby it's turned out to be. We started as a summer replacement and now, because you've all done such a great job, we're in the top ten and assured of a spot on the fall schedule. I'd call that pretty remarkable."

A few people clapped, but it quickly died as everyone waited to hear what Dan was going to say next.

"Fortunately or unfortunately, the network brass thinks you're doing such a great job, I'm not needed around here. There was a drama series I was developing before I got involved with *Sticks and Stones,* and the network would like me to get back to that now that you seem to be on your feet."

"But Dan," Donna Wheeler called from the middle of the crowd, "we haven't had that many episodes on the air. There's a lot more for you to do right here."

Dan looked pained. "I know. I've got a lot of ideas I haven't had a chance to put into effect, but hey, that's the way this business goes. I'm sure Kate will be able to carry out our plans." He glanced over at Kate Morton, the head writer. She smiled weakly.

Ben Epson, who played Joe Stickley, said, "Is Kate going to be our new executive producer?"

"No. Although I told the network Kate would make an excellent choice. They had their own choice, though. Some of you may have heard of him, Randy Ellis."

A small "oh, no" escaped Jamie's lips.

"You know him?" Alison looked at her in alarm.

"I may have been out of the business for a while, but I kept up with the trade papers. Randy Ellis has quite a reputation. He runs his sets like boot camps. He's a real dictator."

Chapter 2

"I think we're supposed to be eating," Alison said unenthusiastically, looking down at her salad.

"Some of us never eat," Mike said pointedly.

Jamie knew the comment was directed at her, but didn't answer.

Alison pushed her plate away. "I just can't believe it. The people at the network must be idiots."

"There had to be some sort of a power play." Mike glanced around the studio cafeteria. "This is such a weird business. Everyone pretending to be your friend, but turn your back for a second and boom! You might just have a knife in it."

Was that for me, too, Mike? Jamie wondered. Mike knew she had tried to sabotage Alison when the show first started, but she'd assumed she had proven herself by now. "Frankly, I'm amazed Dan had so little clout with the network. Even if they insisted on putting him on a new show, he should have been able to veto Randy Ellis."

"What do you know about this Ellis guy?" Mike said, leaning back in his chair. "I've read that he was responsible for firing half the cast on *Next September*."

Jamie nodded. "And he got Robin Aucoin kicked off her show. Donna said she once worked with him and the whole time she felt like she was ducking bullets."

Alison looked a little pale. "Donna's pretty tough. I can't imagine anyone scaring her."

"Imagine it," Jamie replied grimly. "I've got a costume fitting," she said, pushing away her untouched bowl of soup. "I guess I'll see you guys later."

Alison and Mike gave her half-hearted good-byes. "Well, at least we have a week or so until this Randy guy shows up," Alison said. "We can get this show in the can without him breathing down our necks."

"Don't talk about necks," Mike said. He ran a finger across his own.

"I just can't believe he would mess with our success," Alison insisted.

"People like to come in with their own ideas. I may not have been around the business long, but I know that much."

"I think I'm getting depressed." Alison played a little with her salad. This job was the most wonderful, crazy, surprising thing that had ever happened to her. Plucked from obscurity at Madison High School, Alison felt as if she was finally participating in life. And what a life! Glamour and excitement, but even more important, she was turning out to be a pretty good actress. No one was more surprised than Alison that she was actually making a success of this, but now that she was, she'd hate to give any of it up.

Mike shrugged. "All we can do is go with the flow."

"I guess I'm used to things going pretty smoothly," Alison admitted.

Sometimes it embarrassed Alison to think how easy her life had been so far. Being the daughter of a wealthy entertainment lawyer, she had just taken her lovely home, the many vacations, and the support of her parents for granted. Oh, maybe her father had babied her, tried to protect her too much, but that didn't seem like much of a problem now that she realized how other people had to live.

Take Jamie. Her father had deserted his family and they had to work hard in order to make ends meet. She looked speculatively at Mike. What did she know about him? He usually avoided any conversations about his personal life. He lived with some roommates down on Venice Beach. Oh yes, with his dark, brooding eyes and intriguing smile, he was one of the cutest guys she had ever seen. Most people thought her ex-boyfriend was pretty good looking, but Brad D'amato seemed very immature compared to Mike.

"I know your life has gone smoothly. I've been to your house, remember?"

Alison could feel herself blush. "I guess I have been sheltered," she murmured.

"Hey, don't feel guilty about it," Mike advised. "Most us are looking for just the kind of stuff you have."

"I'm glad I'm going to be earning my own way now."

"Really? I would think it would be easier for your father to run the rat race every day."

Alison shook her head. "I want to be doing it myself."

"Well, good for you," Mike said approvingly.

"Let's just hope I can keep doing it. That all of us can."

"I don't think this Randy Ellis is going to ruin the show," Mike replied. "But let's face it, he's not going to make our jobs more fun."

Alison looked at her watch. "I guess we'd better start getting back."

"I wonder how long Dan is going to be around. He was a little vague about that."

"I hope he'll be with us through this show. Did you notice how many lines we have this week?"

"A mixed blessing," Mike said with a laugh. "It's great to be featured, but learning all those lines is going to be murder." He leaned forward. "Say, how would you like to run our lines together this evening?"

Alison could feel her heart start to beat a little faster. *Oh, calm down,* Alison told herself. *It isn't like he's asking you for a date.*

"So what do you say?"

Alison worked very hard at sounding casual. "Sure, why not? Come over around seven." All the while she was thinking, *My parents aren't home from their cruise until tomorrow. We're going to have the house to ourselves.*

Jamie arrived home exhausted. The events of the day had worn her out emotionally and physically. To her surprise, no one was home. After a little searching, she found a note on the kitchen table that said her mother and Elsie had gone to the library.

"Alone at last," she said aloud. Even though she loved her mother and adored Elsie, it was nice to have peace and quiet in the house.

She went into her bedroom, still marveling that she wasn't sleeping on a sofa bed in the living room, the way she had in their old apartment, which was located over a Chinese restaurant.

Flinging her clothes around, Jamie stripped off her turtleneck and jeans. She caught sight of herself, wearing only her underwear, in the closet door mirror.

At first, she was surprised. Her bones were all so prominent, especially around her chest. And speaking of her chest, it seemed to have flattened out. But then Jamie peered more closely. No, her job in the weight-reduction department was hardly finished. She grabbed an inch or so of skin around her waist. "I'm going to have to get rid of these love handles," she said aloud. And her thighs still had a little jiggle to them as well. No, she couldn't stop being vigilant now. If she quit her diet, she'd never get rid of this disgusting fat, and she'd probably put back on every pound she had lost. Well, that wasn't going to happen, Jamie vowed as she went in to take a leisurely bubble bath. She was thin, and she was going to get even thinner.

Jamie was just putting on her robe after soaking for half

an hour when the doorbell rang. Mrs. O'Leary was notorious for forgetting her key, so Jamie didn't think twice about opening the door without checking through the peephole.

"Oh, David!" she gasped.

"Hello, Jamie," David said with a smile.

She could just imagine how she must look in an old robe, her hair piled up in a ratty bun, her eye makeup still a little smeary around her eyes.

"I wasn't expecting company," Jamie stuttered.

"I hope not," David laughed. "I pity any visitor you'd want to see you looking like that."

Jamie's embarrassment disappeared, and righteous indignation took its place. "Well, excuse me. I guess if you had waited for an invitation, you wouldn't have to put up with this horrible sight." Jamie made a move to close the door, but David said, "Hey, don't do that. Can't you change or something while I wait?"

"Why should I?"

"So we can go out to dinner."

Even Jamie had to laugh at that a little. "Fix myself up, so I can spend an evening with someone I'm not even sure I want to spend an hour with. Hey, cool idea."

"I agree, for an hour, I might be difficult to be with, but people find I chill out as the night goes on."

"I don't know if I want to invest an evening checking it out for myself."

David shook his head. "Big mistake, Jamie. Somehow, we've gotten off on the wrong foot, and I just want to straighten things out. Hey, if I'm willing to put up with being seen with a television personality, you should be able to overlook a few of my flaws.''

The ringing phone interrupted them. Jamie threw David a withering glance before going over to answer it.

''Hello?'' She looked at David and then turned away. ''Well, it's great to hear from you, Steve. Tonight? Sure, I can see you tonight. I don't have any plans. Seven? Fine. See you then.''

Jamie hung up, half expecting to see David gone, but no, he was still in the doorway, looking surprisingly unaffected by her grandstand play.

''I guess that means our evening's off?''

''Brilliant deduction, Sherlock. I have a better offer.''

''And who might the lucky guy be?''

''You wouldn't know him.''

''Someone from the show?''

''Someone terrific. Someone who thinks it's exciting to be dating a television star.''

Jamie knew this wasn't true. Steve Kaye was just a nice, sweet guy who liked her. But she wasn't about to tell David that. Let him think that some people enjoyed being seen with a celebrity.

''But Jamie, that's why you need to go out with me. What's the point of going out with someone who's going to make that pretty head of yours even more swollen?''

Jamie saw one of Elsie's plastic glasses sitting on the counter. Without thinking, she threw it toward the door.

David ducked just in time. The glass hit the doorjamb

and fell to the floor. Even this assault wasn't enough to ruffle David. He picked it up and placed it on the kitchen counter. "Perhaps another evening." With a little bow and a slight smile, he turned and left.

"Good riddance," Jamie muttered, trying to ignore the small pang that she felt as the door closed.

Determined to put David out of her mind, Jamie went upstairs to dress for her date. If she had Alison to thank for one thing, it was introducing her to Steve. He used to spend most of his time pursuing Alison's friend, Dana, to no avail. Then he'd asked Jamie to his prom, and she'd had a surprisingly good time.

Steve is who you should be dating, Jamie told herself as she slipped into a short plaid miniskirt and bright red T-shirt. Nice, sweet, not a major-league creep like David. He ought to star in a movie called *The Irritator.*

By the time Jamie finished wrapping a black-and-red scarf around her neck and adding lots of silver bracelets to her wrist, Mrs. O'Leary and Elsie were home.

"Jamie, you look so pretty," Elsie exclaimed.

"Thanks, baby."

"When I was your age, redheads were told never to wear the color red. On you, it looks great. But, Jamie," her mother added worriedly, "aren't you losing too much weight?"

"I told you, I was looking too heavy on camera." Jamie had come to half believe the story she was telling.

"Maybe when you first started, but surely not now."

"Just a few more pounds, Mom, that's all I need to take off."

Before her mother could protest, Jamie said, "I think I hear Steve honking."

"I didn't hear anything," Elsie said innocently.

Jamie just kissed her on the head, grabbed her purse, and headed outside.

Steve drove up as she came out the door. "Hi," she said gaily, as she slid into his new, very cool sports car.

"I would have come in. You can't still be embarrassed about where you live. This place looks nice."

Steve was one of the few people who knew how Jamie's former address humiliated her.

"Oh, it is. And I was going to wait inside, except my mother was getting on my case."

"What about?"

"The usual," Jamie said vaguely. She didn't want to talk about her weight. Fortunately, at the Italian restaurant, Steve seemed so interested in the conversation, he didn't notice Jamie pushing her pasta around her plate. Unlike David, Steve was fascinated by life at the studio and her trip to New York. Jamie had a terrific time, but when they headed out for a ride in the mountains after dinner, Jamie began to feel uncomfortable. She looked over at Steve. Thin and wiry, with short, black hair and glasses, Steve's cuteness came mostly from his terrific personality. She knew he was headed up to one of the mountain drives where the main activity was making out.

Jamie didn't know what to do. Did she feel like doing the girlfriend thing with him?

"Steve, I've got an early call tomorrow."

"Oh, it's not that late." He pulled over to a spot with a

sparkling view of the city below. Casually, he put his arm around her.

Jamie felt guilty. The only reason she was up here was because she was trying to get back at David. Now it looked as if her selfishness was going to hurt Steve.

"Steve . . ."

"Don't talk." He leaned over and kissed her.

Like Steve, the kiss was very sweet, but Jamie couldn't honestly say it stirred anything inside her. When Steve pulled away, he smiled at her, and Jamie smiled weakly back.

Steve wasn't a sensitive guy for nothing. "All right, so it wasn't the Fourth of July, but remember, even fireworks start with a spark."

Jamie laughed.

"Do you want to try it again?"

"Not right now," Jamie said, "but I wouldn't mind practicing sometime." She was being sensible, she told herself. Her relationship with David was so up and down. There was no reason to discourage a perfectly good guy like Steve just because she wasn't in a full-blown swoon.

"Then we can go out again?" Steve asked eagerly.

"Sure." Why not? Her social calendar had plenty of room.

As she got ready to go to bed, Jamie tried to dismiss all the thoughts that were crowding her brain: work, Randy, David, Steve. She tried especially hard not to compare the few kisses she had shared with David to the one this evening.

Punching her pillow, Jamie consoled herself with the thought that at least things hadn't worked out too badly with Steve. Would all the changes at *Sticks and Stones* go as well? Somehow, Jamie doubted it.

Chapter 3

"I can't believe it. You've totally humiliated me!" Alison could feel the tears crowding her eyes. She hurried out of the Blakes' family room and headed upstairs.

"Alison, you can't just leave. Now come back here," her father said insistently.

Alison hesitated. She might be mad, but she wasn't used to disobeying a direct order from her father. Reluctantly, she returned and flopped down on the couch. "All right, I'm here," she said defiantly.

Mrs. Blake looked at her daughter wonderingly. "We've been gone less than two weeks. It's like we're coming home to a changed daughter."

"Maybe I've just learned to stand up for myself. It took me long enough."

Her parents seemed shocked at her attitude, and Alison had to admit that she was just as surprised. Maybe more so. But a little back talk was nothing compared to the way they had treated her.

It all began with what Alison thought was going to be the most wonderful evening of her life. Never had she been so excited about a date with Brad as she was about just going over lines with Mike. Because it was the housekeeper's night off, she planned to make Mike dinner herself.

Not that her cooking repertoire was all that extensive. Mike had come over once before, and she had made him grilled cheese sandwiches. All that left was her scrambled eggs and toast. Alison had visions of herself serving Mike his dinner—even though it was more like breakfast—as he sat at the kitchen table smiling up at her.

It hadn't turned out that way at all. Mike had come in hungry, all right, but he made a face when she suggested eggs.

"Sorry, but they're so squishy and yellow . . . and when you think where they came from . . ."

"I get the picture," Alison said, making a face. "But," she added with embarrassment, "I don't know how to make much else. You've had my grilled cheese. Will a peanut butter and jelly sandwich be okay?"

"Can I look in your cupboards?" Mike asked.

Alison nodded.

"Good . . . great!" he said, surveying the contents. Mike turned to Alison. "I'll make dinner," he informed her.

Alison could hardly believe this was the motorcycle fiend standing at the stove whipping up a tuna-noodle casserole. As he shoved it into the oven, Mike said, "Okay, let's run some lines while it cooks."

Alison laughed. "A chef one minute, TV actor the next. You are one talented guy."

Mike took a little bow. "Thank you."

"Where did you learn to cook?" Alison asked as they settled themselves at the kitchen table.

"My roommates and I take turns," Mike replied with a shrug.

"Who are your roommates?" Alison asked. "You never really said."

"Oh, just two other struggling young thespians," Mike said vaguely. He opened to page one of the script. "Want to start?"

While the casserole bubbled away in the oven, sending heavenly smells throughout the kitchen, Alison and Mike went over their lines. Alison felt she had never done a better job with a script. It was pretty clear that working one-on-one with Mike was inspiring her. Finally they had to quit. "I'm famished," Alison said. "How much longer to dinner?"

Mike checked his watch. "It's ready now."

Alison set the table with festive china and her mom's prettiest napkins. At the last minute she decided to add some candles, hoping she wasn't being too forward.

"Hey, nice touch," Mike said. "I hope this goop can live up to the ambience."

"It looks wonderful," Alison protested. "And we've got a salad in the refrigerator and these rolls that Estelle made. I think it's as good as any meal we had in New York," Alison declared stoutly.

"Wait 'til you taste it," Mike responded dryly.

Actually, Alison barely noticed the food at all. There was a fluttery feeling in her stomach that pushed out all other sensations. All she could think about was the wonderful kiss Mike had given her in New York. Would there be more kisses tonight?

"Shall we do the dishes?" Mike asked when they finished.

"I'll just rinse them off. Estelle has her own way of putting them in the dishwasher."

Together they quickly cleared the table. At the sink, Alison ran water over one of the glasses, when she felt a small brushing sensation against the back of her neck. Surprised, she turned her head and almost bumped noses with Mike, who was caressing her shoulder.

"Oh!"

"You just look so sweet standing there."

"Washing dishes?" Alison asked with a nervous laugh.

"You look pretty sweet no matter what you're doing," Mike responded softly. He took the glass out of her hand. "Let's go sit down somewhere, can we?"

Almost in a trance, Alison led Mike into the family room. They sat down on the soft leather sofa, and Mike gently took her hand. "You know this could complicate things."

"I know."

"Ever since New York I've been trying to tell myself this would be a bad idea. Getting involved with a co-worker is hardly ever smart," Mike said.

"We never talked about those . . . kisses. I thought maybe it was a mistake."

"I tried to convince myself of that, too, Ali. But when I see you, at the studio, or even washing dishes, looking so pretty . . ."

"Oh, Mike, quit teasing."

"I wish I were. It's hard to concentrate on anything but you, Alison."

"I know what you mean," Alison murmured.

"Sometimes, I feel like I just want to take you in my arms." Gently, he drew her closer to him. "And kiss you one more time."

Alison was lost as Mike's lips lingered on hers. She never heard the front door open. The first thing she heard was her mother's voice.

"Alison, we're home."

Both Alison and Mike jerked up, startled and embarrassed.

"I didn't hear you come in," Alison said, clearing her throat.

"Apparently not."

"Hello, Mr. and Mrs. Blake," Mike said, rising.

Mr. Blake nodded at him curtly. "Where's Estelle?" he asked.

"She's off for the evening," Alison said, trying to sound casual. From the surprised looks on her parents' faces, she could tell she wasn't pulling it off.

"So you're here alone," Mr. Blake said.

"Yes. Did you have a good time on your trip?" Alison asked, desperate to change the subject.

Her mother came to her rescue. "Yes, we did. It was lovely, wasn't it, Peter?"

Mr. Blake nodded.

"We have so much to tell each other," Mrs. Blake continued with forced gaiety. "Shall I put up some coffee, and we can trade stories?"

"I think I'd better go, Mrs. Blake," Mike said. "Alison and I were going over our new script, but I guess we've finished."

"Yes, you have," Mr. Blake said.

"I'll walk you out," Alison said. "I didn't know they were coming home tonight," she whispered as they moved toward the door. "They were supposed to come home tomorrow morning."

"Are they going to give you a hard time?" Mike asked worriedly. "Maybe I should stay."

"No, no. I think they were just surprised."

"All right, then. I'll see you tomorrow." He patted her awkwardly on the shoulder.

Great, Alison thought. *Just great. What could have been the most romantic evening of my life just ended with a pat on the shoulder.* Angrily, she marched back into the family room.

"Alison . . ." her father began.

"We weren't doing anything wrong!"

"No one said you were," Mrs. Blake, ever the peacemaker, interjected, "but you know you're not supposed to have boys over when no one is home."

"I'm going to be sixteen next month."

"All the more reason," her father muttered. "Besides, that kid is way too old for you."

"He's a couple of years older."

"And decades more savvy."

"You don't give me very much credit. And you made pretty sure that Mike knows you don't trust him either."

"Well, why should I trust him?" her father blew up.

That's when Alison had stalked out of the room. Now that she'd been forced back to the couch, Alison was determined not to say anything. Let her father rant and rave if he wanted. The evening couldn't get much worse.

But before Alison's father could say anything, Mrs. Blake spoke up. "Now, before we all go crazy here, let's calm down. Your father and I are exhausted. We've had a very long flight, and I don't think any of us is ready for an argument."

"What are you doing home so early, anyway?" Alison muttered.

"We caught an early flight so we could get home to see you," Mrs. Blake said.

"We didn't expect to find you nuzzling on the couch with some man," Mr. Blake added.

"Peter . . ." his wife warned.

"All right, all right."

"Alison, you know the rules," Mrs. Blake said. "You really shouldn't have had Mike here when you were alone."

"Okay, okay, I apologize," Alison said wearily.

"Then let's shelve this particular discussion until tomorrow," her mother said. "Now, tell us, how was your trip to New York?"

Alison didn't feel like segueing into a bunch of anecdotes about her trip, but anything was better than having a fight with her parents on their first night back. Hesitantly, she began telling them about all the exciting things that had happened to her. The more she told, the more she warmed to her subject. By the time she had brought them up to date on the talk shows, the modeling assignment, and the glamour of the American Choice Awards, she was feeling pretty normal.

"I'm so glad we have it all on tape," Mrs. Blake said. "I'd feel terrible if I missed this."

"I don't know if I want you to see my interview on the *Today* show. It was pretty dismal. I was really making a mess of all my interviews until Jamie, Rodney, and Mike helped me out. So, tell me about your trip."

"Not tonight," said Mrs. Blake. "I'm just too tired. But tomorrow, I'll tell you everything. I can't wait to show you all the things we got you."

"Maybe we should go to bed now," Alison agreed. "I've got an early call."

"I'm sorry our homecoming got off to such a bad start." Mrs. Blake looked at her husband, who grudgingly nodded.

"I am, too, Mom. I am too."

Alison knew she must look terrible this morning. She hadn't slept at all. When she wasn't tossing and turning, worrying about whether Mike was totally turned off by her, she was thinking about Randy Ellis and how his presence would change her life. By the time she stumbled into the limo, Alison felt as if even a total makeover wouldn't be enough of a help.

"Good morning," she said to Jamie, as she got into the car.

"Boy, you look a little bleary-eyed," Jamie commented.

"It shows?"

"Don't worry. That's why we've got a makeup department."

Wearily, Alison laid her head against the seat. "They're going to be earning their salaries on me today."

"So what's wrong?" Jamie inquired.

Alison hesitated. Was there any chance she could discuss last night with Jamie? Since she and Dana had had a falling out, Alison really didn't have a girlfriend to share secrets with. She was very tempted, but couldn't quite bring herself to confide about Mike.

Instead she said, "I'm afraid I've had Randy Ellis on my mind."

"Who hasn't?"

"I hate surprises," Alison said vehemently.

Jamie looked at Alison in surprise. What was going on here? Alison was usually so even-tempered.

"What's new with you?" Alison asked, desperate to get the subject off herself.

Jamie wondered if she should tell Alison about her date with Steve. She was tired of not having anyone to talk to. "I went out with Steve last night."

"Did you? Good!"

Jamie sighed. "He wants to be more than friends."

"So?"

"There's this other guy, I think I mentioned him."

Alison laughed. "To quote you, that would be 'David the jerk' or 'David, Mr. Pompous' or 'David who thinks he's better than anyone.' *He's* the one you like?"

Jamie had to laugh along with her. "He drives me crazy, but he's awfully cute."

"Gee, I thought maybe something might develop between you and Steve. Did you really give it a chance?"

That question made Jamie pause. Had she? "I've only had two dates with him."

"And you had a good time? I know you did at the prom."

"Yeah, I did, but . . ."

"But no bells went off?"

"Not one," Jamie answered.

"Sometimes it takes time to hear bells."

Jamie wondered if Alison was right. "I said I'd still see him. Heck, I don't even know if I'll hear from David again."

"So, no problem." Alison realized she was enjoying this conversation with Jamie. Maybe she should have told her what happened with Mike last night after all. She didn't think the chemistry would ever be right between her and Jamie.

But all thoughts of boys flew out of Jamie's mind when she reached the set. Yesterday, there had been an air of nervous anticipation. Today the mood was downright dread.

Cindy Vargas, the production assistant who had accompanied them on their trip to New York, came up to Jamie and Alison as they walked through the door.

"He's here!" she hissed.

Jamie looked taken aback. "Randy? Already?"

Cindy nodded. "He's observing this week. He wants to meet you guys."

"Well, I don't suppose we have much choice," Alison said, trying to stand a little straighter.

"Hardly. He's waiting for you in his office."

Alison had thought that the first thing she was going to have to endure this morning was apologizing for her parents to Mike. That little episode would seem like a picnic compared to walking into the lion's den. She had to admit she was awfully glad that Jamie was coming with her. Jamie knew how to stand up for herself.

But Jamie wasn't feeling very courageous herself. *What if this guy hates me*, she thought. Visions of all her newfound success disappearing crowded her mind.

It hadn't taken long for Randy to clear out Dan's office and make it his own. Already, Dan's artwork and desk accessories were gone, and a poster from one of Randy's successful television shows hung askew on the wall.

Randy himself sat behind Dan's desk. A tall man with thinning dark hair, Randy's look was intense as the girls walked into the room.

"Alison Blake and Jamie O'Leary," he said before Cindy could introduce them. She quickly disappeared out the door.

"Have a seat," he said curtly.

When the girls were settled, he said, "I'm just meeting the cast and crew today. Then I'll be observing on the set.

I want to get some idea of how things are going around here.''

There was a silence that finally Jamie felt obligated to fill. ''I think things are going pretty well. We are in the top ten, after all.''

''Yes. But that doesn't mean there isn't room for improvement. I've been screening the shows that have been shot so far. I think the quality of writing could use some improvement.''

Alison and Jamie exchanged glances. Kate Morton was one of the best writers in the business. If Randy wasn't happy with her work, what chance did the rest of them have?

''What about the acting?'' Jamie asked boldly.

''There's always room for improvement in any endeavor.'' He turned to Alison. ''I understand you're a novice in the business.''

''That's right.''

''Don't you find that rather nerve-racking?''

''Sometimes,'' Alison said quietly.

''Alison's one of the most popular cast members on the show.'' Even Jamie was surprised to hear herself leap to Alison's defense. But there was something about this guy that made her want to tangle with him. *Restrain yourself, girl,* she told herself. *The last thing you want to do is get on the wrong side of your executive producer. Especially in the cause of Alison Blake.*

''Well, I want everyone to know I'm going to be a hands-on producer. I'm sure you won't mind that.''

''That's certainly your prerogative,'' Alison said.

"Thank you for that, my dear."

Alison couldn't tell whether he was being sarcastic.

"I guess that's all for now," Randy said dismissively. "I'll see you two on the set."

Alison and Jamie departed, relieved that the audience had ended. "So how do you think it went?" Alison asked, once they were out of earshot.

Jamie shook her head. "I think Randy Ellis is out gunning. And I think it's for us."

Chapter 4

"Where are you and Mike going tonight?" Mrs. Blake ran her finger over the quilting on Alison's bedspread.

"I'm not sure."

"Alison, you know your dad and I like to know your plans."

Through gritted teeth, Alison said, "To a movie, I guess. Would you like me to call you when I get there and tell you what time it lets out?"

Mrs. Blake shook her head. "I'm not used to sarcasm from you, Ali."

"I'm sorry, Mom, really, but I don't understand what the big deal is. You never objected to Brad, and Mike's much nicer."

"Really?" Mrs. Blake looked surprised. "You never talked much about why you and Brad broke up. Was there something about him you didn't like?"

Alison didn't know how much she wanted to confide in her mother. In years past, she had shared just about everything, but Alison didn't feel the urge to do that anymore. Maybe that's what growing up meant, not having to tell Mommy and Daddy everything.

Alison was sure that nothing matured you faster than being on a network television show. Sometimes, she felt just as pressured as any other adult holding down a responsible job. Though her parents certainly tried to draw her out about the show, it was something she didn't talk about too much. Why, she hadn't even told them about Randy Ellis. She had mentioned Dan was gone and that Randy was always around, but she hadn't said a word about how everyone on the set was nervously looking over his shoulder. So far all Randy had done was stand stony-faced on the set during rehearsals and at the taping, but that had been enough. It changed the whole mood of the show.

"Was there something about Brad you didn't tell us?" her mother persisted.

"Not really. He was just too possessive. He hated the idea of me being on television."

"I guess that's a problem you won't have with Mike."

"I do have a lot more in common with him," Alison agreed.

Mr. Blake stuck his head in the doorway. "Alison, I'd like to talk to Mike before you and he go out this evening."

Alison looked at her father, horrified. "About what?"

"I'd just like to get to know him a little better," Mr. Blake answered blandly.

"Dad, sitting down with the new boyfriend, that's something out of the Dark Ages."

"Clare, I do believe it's getting a little dark in here," Mr. Blake joked.

Alison didn't think it was all that funny. "You're going to ruin this for me." She could hear her voice rising.

"Alison," her mother said calmly, "if Mike doesn't want to talk to your parents for a few minutes, I'd say this relationship is already on pretty shaky ground."

"It isn't on any ground yet."

They were interrupted by the doorbell.

"That's Mike," Alison said.

"You finish getting dressed," her father said. "Your mother and I will get it."

Alison dressed in record speed. The last thing she wanted was Mike subjected to one of her father's interrogations. Mr. Blake was a top attorney. If there was one thing he knew how to do, it was ask questions.

By the time Alison got downstairs, her parents were chatting away with Mike in the family room. She stood unnoticed and watched for a few moments. He was pushing a lock of dark hair away from his forehead, a gesture that Alison had come to recognize as nervousness, but that was the only thing that betrayed him. Alison had intended to stop her parents pronto, but Mike seemed to be handling the "interview" pretty well, so Alison held back.

You shouldn't eavesdrop, she told herself, but she backed out of the line of vision and listened in on the conversation.

"How old are you, Mike?" her father asked.

"I'll be nineteen next month."

"You know, Alison is only fifteen," Mrs. Blake said.

I'm going to be sixteen next month, Alison wanted to yell, but she held her tongue.

"Yes," Mike said politely.

Mr. Blake looked back coolly. "That's something of a difference at this age, don't you think?"

"Maybe, if Alison was a regular high-school student, and I was in college, but right now, Alison and I are co-workers."

Good answer, Alison cheered silently.

"Well, that's another issue," Mr. Blake continued. "Do you really think it's smart to be dating a co-worker?"

Mike spent a little longer pondering this question. "I can see where it could cause problems, but heck, Mr. Blake, this is Alison's and my first date. I think it's too early to worry about how this is going to turn out."

"Maybe not," Mr. Blake disagreed bluntly.

"That's it," Alison muttered. She strode into the family room. "Hi, Mike. I think we'd better get going if we want to make a movie."

"Are you going to a show in Westwood?" Mrs. Blake asked.

Mike rose. "I have a newspaper in the car. There are so many theaters in Westwood, I'm sure we'll find something."

"Alison, remember your curfew," her mother said.

"I will. Good night." She couldn't wait to close the door behind her.

"Whew," Mike said, pretending to wipe his brow.

"So it *was* bad. You looked so cool, I couldn't tell if it was getting to you or not."

"Let's just say it's been a while since I've been quizzed about my motives like that."

"I'm so sorry," Alison whispered.

"Hey, it's okay. Your parents have a right to know who you're going out with. You are only fifteen, after all."

"I'm going to be sixteen next month!" Alison declared loudly. Then she clapped her hand over her mouth and giggled. "Sorry, I'm tired of being accused of being fifteen."

"Got you," Mike said with a smile.

They stopped in front of a new jeep.

"Your new car!" Alison squealed with delight.

"Yep. Isn't it a beauty?"

Alison walked around the car admiring it. "But what about your motorcycle?" she asked. She knew he was passionate about his Harley.

"Oh, I'll never give that up. I'll take you on it sometime. Maybe when your parents trust me a little more."

"Good thinking," Alison said, as she slid into the front seat. She didn't think she was ready to fight the battle of the two-wheeler this evening.

As Mike pulled out of the driveway, Alison said, "You know, I always thought I was lucky. When the other girls complained about their parents, I kept my mouth shut. My father was overprotective, but he could lighten up when I needed him to. I've never seen him like this."

"He's never seen you with me," Mike replied shrewdly.

Alison could feel her heart twirling a little at Mike's husky tone. "I hope my parents weren't too much of a turn-off," she finally said quietly.

Mike reached over and took her hand. "It would take more than a short inquisition to turn me off of you."

Well, another big Saturday night, Jamie thought as she leafed through the *TV Guide. I wonder what's on television.*

"What are you doing?" Elsie asked, climbing up on the couch.

"Just checking out the shows."

"The Cosby Show's going to come on soon," Elsie informed her. "It's got Rudy and Vanessa . . ."

"Thank you, but I don't think I'm in the mood for a rerun tonight. Especially a sitcom. I work on one all day, you know."

"What are you in the mood for?" Elsie asked seriously.

"Oh, dancing at a fancy nightclub with a very cool companion."

"You can come to dinner with Mommy and Daddy and me at McDonald's."

Jamie laughed. "That's not exactly what I had in mind."

Mrs. O'Leary came out of the kitchen. "You might enjoy being with your family," she said pointedly.

Jamie didn't take the bait. The last thing she wanted to do was get into a discussion about spending more time with her father. He had been a little better lately, but that didn't mean she wanted to do the family thing with him. "Maybe some other time."

Mrs. O'Leary shrugged in resignation. "Your father will be here any minute, Elsie. Come on, you have to get ready."

Elsie hopped off the couch. "Okay," she said agreeably.

Not for the first time, Jamie wished she had a little bit of her sister's easy disposition.

Clicking on the television, she roamed from one channel to the next, but nothing caught her attention. She was almost glad when her father arrived, allowing her to turn off the darn thing.

"How are you doing, Jamie?" Mr. O'Leary asked almost shyly.

"Okay. Mom and Elsie will be right out." She looked at her father critically. He looked better than usual. What was it? "You have a new haircut."

Mr. O'Leary laughed with embarrassment. "Yeah, I went to one of those stylists, and she parted it a little differently. 'Course, I don't have enough hair to make much of a difference."

"Sure you do," Jamie said. "And that sweater is new, too, isn't it?" It was better than anything she had ever seen him in.

"Yeah, now that I've got a little money to spend, I bought a few things."

Jamie looked at him suspiciously. "Did you win at the track or something?"

"No. I got a job."

"A job!"

"You know I've been looking, Jamie. Well, something finally came through."

"Something in show business?"

"Sort of. I'm going to be working at a local television station, selling time."

"You mean, companies come to you and buy commercial time on TV shows?"

Mr. O'Leary nodded. "Only right now, I'm selling the late-night spots, so there's not much commission. But it's a start."

"Well, that's good, Dad." Jamie was surprised to see how easily she offered her congratulations. "Have you told Mom yet?"

"Nope. Over dinner. She thinks we're going to McDonald's, but I have something a little nicer in mind." Mr. O'Leary cleared his throat. "Are you sure you won't join us? I'd like this to be a family celebration."

Jamie was tempted, but saying no was such a habit that she just shook her head no. "Maybe some other time, Dad. I'm exhausted."

Her father's face fell, but he said, "I understand."

"Thanks," she said sincerely.

Once they had left, Jamie wondered if she had made a mistake by not joining them. She curled up on the couch thinking about her trip to New York. That had been so much fun, so glamorous. What a comedown this was.

You're feeling sorry for yourself, she thought, blinking back a few tears. She was also very tired, as she told her father. Maybe the best thing to do would be just climb into bed, no matter how early it was.

As she was dragging herself toward the bedroom, Jamie heard a noise on the front walk. Nervously, she peeked out the window. "Oh, no."

There was David. He wasn't doing anything, he was just standing there, his back to the door.

"Well, I'm not going to invite him in," Jamie said determinedly. Then she flung open the door. "What are you doing lurking around my house?"

For once, David looked embarrassed. "Oh, hi."

"Oh, hi? That's it?"

"I was trying to decide whether to ring the bell."

Maybe she would like some company. She opened the door wider. "Well, don't just stand there. The neighbors are going to start talking. Come on in."

Once inside, David seemed even more uncomfortable. "So what are you up to, Jamie?" he asked, as if he had just run into her on the street.

"If you had arrived a few minutes later, you would have found me in my pajamas."

Now David grinned. "Bathrobe, pajamas—this could become a habit."

"Don't get any big ideas, David." She walked into the kitchen. "Want a Coke or something?"

"Sure."

Jamie poured a couple of diet colas and brought them over to the kitchen table where David had made himself comfortable.

"So, Jamie, how was your date the other night?"

"Fine."

"Who was the lucky guy?" David asked, taking a sip of his drink.

"Someone who went to high school with Alison Blake. Steve Kaye."

"Not someone from the studio?" David looked surprised.

"You think I only date big shots? Stars of tomorrow?" *You should only know.*

"It would make sense."

"Not to me," Jamie bristled. "Steve is a nice guy." No need to enlighten David further about her relationship with Steve.

"That's good," David said, smiling again. "Gives me hope."

"So how's your career going?" Jamie said, wanting to get off the subject of Steve.

"Let's put it like this, you're not the only working actor in the room."

Jamie was pleased in spite of herself. "Really? You got a gig?"

"I did."

"Let's see, it can't be on a soap. Maybe you're going to be wearing the Mickey Mouse suit at Disneyland?"

David took the teasing gracefully. "I think Donald Duck is more my style, but no. I'm going to be doing a little Shakespeare."

"Wow. But do you think he's worthy of your talent?"

"I think Shakespeare and I make a great combination," David replied loftily.

"So where is all this drama going to take place?"

"Actually, it's a comedy, *The Taming of the Shrew.* And the production is going to be at the Santa Monica Playhouse."

Jamie had to admit she was impressed. The Playhouse was a small theater, but it had a good reputation, especially for doing avant-garde versions of classics. "What part did you get?"

"Well, I'm not Kate, and I'm not Petruchio. But I am one of his friends. I think I'll really get into it."

David became animated as he explained the role to Jamie and what he thought he could do with it, and she couldn't help but respond. Maybe David was a snob about acting, but she knew how it felt to be taken over by a character. Jamie could understand and respect that.

"Hey, I've been yammering away and haven't let you say a word," David finally broke off. "How are things at *Sticks and Stones*?"

Jamie was about to make a smart remark about it not being Shakespeare, but suddenly she realized she wouldn't mind telling David about what was going on at the show. She and the rest of the cast had talked the topic practically into the ground, but it might be nice to get an outsider's opinion. "There's some trouble, actually," she began.

"Want to tell me about it over a hamburger?" David interrupted. "I'm getting hungry. Past my dinnertime."

Jamie didn't want a hamburger, and just the thought of one made her snappish. "Not really."

David was taken aback. "Excuse me. I was only inviting you out to eat."

"I . . . I'm not feeling well." If there was one thing Jamie could do, it was think of a lie and think of it quickly. "I might have a touch of the stomach flu."

Immediately, David's expression turned to concern. "Why didn't you say something? I'm bending your ear, and you probably want to crawl into bed. No wonder you were getting into your pajamas."

Darn, darn, darn, Jamie thought. David was getting up to leave, and to her amazement, that was the last thing she wanted him to do.

"You don't have to go," she said, following him into the living room. "I'm just not up for food. I could make you something, though."

"You don't want to stand over a stove if you're feeling lousy. I can grab something later. But I'll stay for a while if you're sure you want company."

Jamie nodded. Just as she was about to join David on the couch, there was a knock at the door.

"Are you expecting someone else?" David asked.

"I wasn't expecting you, remember?" she replied tartly, as she opened the door. "Steve!"

"Hi, Jamie. I know I should have called, but I was just driving around and wound up here. Are you . . ." He caught sight of David frowning on the couch. "I guess you are busy."

Jamie didn't know whether to laugh or to cry. What was the etiquette for this situation? She couldn't leave

Steve standing in the doorway looking dumb. "Come in, I'd like you to meet my friend, David. He's an actor, too," she added inanely.

While Jamie made the introductions, Steve and David shook hands, each looking at the other like he was yesterday's dinner.

"So," Jamie said as they settled themselves.

Steve and David didn't say anything.

Racking her brain, Jamie tried to think of a topic they could all talk about. Smiling brightly, she leaned forward and said enthusiastically, "What about those Dodgers?"

Chapter 5

Alison didn't know when she had felt so close to Jamie. After weeks of tense conversations and misunderstandings, here were the two co-stars, in the limo on the way to work, talking like friends.

She supposed they had Randy Ellis to thank for their newfound closeness. Like students under the eye of a frowning teacher, Alison and Jamie found reasons to huddle together and vent their feelings about how unfair Randy was.

At first, most of their conversations had been worried discussions about what Randy would mean to the show in general and to them in particular. But during their car rides to the studio, talk sometimes veered to the personal. Jamie found herself telling Alison about her weekend, just like any other girlfriend.

"So there they were, both of them just sitting in your living room?" Alison asked.

"Glaring at each other," Jamie said, smiling a little.

"And it wasn't horrible?"

"No, actually, it was kind of fun."

"Boy, you must have nerves of steel. I would have run upstairs and put my head under the pillow."

Jamie shrugged and settled back against the plush limo seat. "They acted like gentlemen. Mostly. In his nice way, Steve got in a few digs. He mentioned that he was going to be applying to Stanford for pre-med. And he talked a lot about the great time we had at the prom."

"What did David do?"

Jamie laughed. "He kept trying to steer the conversation back to acting."

"So how did the evening end?" Alison asked.

"With me sending them home about an hour later."

"Arguing all the way?"

"Out the door at least. I couldn't even get them to agree on how the Dodgers were going to do this year."

Alison looked at Jamie. "Does this mean you're going to give Steve another chance?"

"It is kind of fun to have two guys wanting me," Jamie admitted. "And Steve is certainly a sweetheart."

"What about David?" Alison asked shrewdly.

"David mixes me up," Jamie confessed. "He's bugging the heck out of me one minute and totally adorable the next."

"Hey, then go for it. There's no law that says you have to date just one guy."

Jamie cocked her head. "What about you? Are you dating anyone special?"

Alison wasn't sure how much she should say. It was

fine to hear Jamie's confidences, but did she want to get into her relationship with Mike? Alison was pretty sure that Jamie was over her own feelings for Mike—anyway, she probably didn't have room in her living room for one more guy—but Alison and Mike had decided last Saturday to keep their dating under wraps for a while.

"Maybe your dad does have a point," Mike had said while they were having a pizza after the movie. "Dating a co-worker can be rough."

"Does that mean our first date is our last date?" Alison asked quietly.

"No, no." Mike grabbed her hand. "But we should keep this to ourselves for a while. I don't mind secrets, do you?"

"Not this one," she had replied.

Now, though, sitting with Jamie, she wanted to confide just a little.

Looking at Jamie searchingly, she began, "If I tell you something, do you promise . . ."

"You and Mike?" Jamie guessed.

Alison couldn't help the smile that spread across her face. "It was just one date, and I had the best time. But we don't want people at the studio to know."

"I get it. Loose lips sink ships."

"Or careers, anyway."

"Well, no one will hear it from me," Jamie vowed.

"You don't mind? About Mike and me, I mean."

"Oh, maybe there's a little pang somewhere deep down," Jamie admitted, "but I think you and Mike are a lot more suited to each other."

''It was only a date.'' Alison felt she had to remind herself of this as much as Jamie.

As they pulled up to the studio Jamie said with a sigh, ''Coming to work isn't as much fun as it used to be.''

''I wonder what King Randy has in store for us this week.''

It didn't take them long to find out. They hadn't been in the dressing room five minutes when Cindy came in followed by a girl about their own age. She had olive skin and dark hair that fell into curls down to her shoulders.

''Jamie, Alison, this is Shana Ellis.''

''Ellis?'' Jamie inquired, cocking an eyebrow.

''I'm Randy's niece,'' Shana said with just a touch of embarrassment.

''Shana's going to be on the show,'' Cindy informed them.

''Gee, I wonder how you got the job,'' Jamie said, not trying to hide the sting in her voice.

''Hey, don't hold my uncle against me.''

Jamie shrugged. Alison wasn't much happier than Jamie, but she didn't feel like she could just be rude to this girl. ''What part will you be playing, Shana?''

''Devon Anderson. Your next-door neighbor.''

''That's cozy,'' Jamie said.

Alison shook her head at Jamie. ''Welcome to *Sticks and Stones*,'' she said, trying to sound pleasant.

The second Shana and Cindy were out the door, Jamie exploded. ''I can't believe it! Now he's hiring relatives?''

''It's not Shana's fault.''

''There are already too many Ellises on this show,''
Jamie fumed. ''We don't need another one.''

''What can we do about it?''

Jamie sat down on the couch. ''Not much,'' she admitted, deflated.

Alison checked her watch. ''It's time for the run-
through.''

Mondays used to be the most fun day of the week, sitting around, reading the script aloud for the first time, but
it wasn't today. Randy sat at the head of the table, wearing
a perpetual frown. Dan used to let the director, Kevin
Voight, make suggestions to the cast about the way they
should read their parts, but Randy seemed to want to do
that himself. Instead of phrasing his comments helpfully,
he said things like, ''Alison, you sound like a wet noodle.
Can we get a little life into this thing?'' Or, ''Mike, your
looks aren't going to get you through this scene. Try acting.''

By the time the session was over, the cast felt as if they
had run a marathon, not run through some lines.

''That man is insufferable,'' Donna said, grabbing her
script when Randy finally called a lunch break.

Ben was more philosophical. ''He hasn't fired anybody.''

''Yet,'' Donna countered.

''Shall we grab some lunch?'' Mike whispered to Alison.

''I guess,'' she said listlessly.

''Is he getting to you, Alison?''

"My confidence is melting like ice cream on a hot day."

"The problem is Randy's," Mike said forcefully, "not yours."

Alison shrugged. "Before we go to lunch, I said I'd check in with Cindy. She said she has some fan mail for me."

"See, somebody out there likes you." Mike smiled down at her. "And someone standing next to you does, too."

"Thanks," Alison said, perking up a little.

They walked over to Cindy's office. "Hi, you guys," she greeted them. "How did things go?"

"Randy has a problem with us," Alison said. "He thinks we stink."

"Oh, Alison, I'm sure you're exaggerating."

"Not really," Mike said dryly.

Cindy sighed. "Oh, for the good old days. Like last week." She pointed to a pile of canvas bags in the corner of the room. "There's something that should perk you up, though. Alison, your fan mail."

"All that!" Alison exclaimed. "Am I supposed to answer it?"

"The studio will help," Cindy informed her.

"Didn't I get any?" Mike asked.

Cindy laughed. "Don't panic. The mail room hasn't finished sorting." Cindy handed Alison a manila envelope. "I pulled out some at random so you could have a look."

"Thanks," Alison said. "Maybe this will change my opinion of myself."

After Alison and Mike had settled themselves with two hamburgers, Alison opened the envelope.

"You want to read those now?" Mike said, taking a bite of his burger.

"Maybe one or two." She opened the first letter and scanned it. "Oh, this one's nice. A woman from Kansas City is in a hospital, and she says having the show to look forward to perks up her whole week." Alison read another one. "A girl from Montana wants to know if I color my hair." Alison smiled up at Mike. "She also says you're way cool and thinks I should make a play for you."

"And you did."

Alison swatted him with the letter.

Mike reached over and picked up another envelope. It was dirty gray, as if it had been in someone's drawer for a long time. "Here's someone with a small stationery budget."

Alison made a face at Mike, pulled the letter away from him, and started reading. Her eyes widened, then she hurriedly stuffed it back in its envelope.

"What did that one say?"

"Nothing.

"C'mon, Ali, you looked a little sick while you were reading it."

Alison hesitated. "It wasn't very nice."

Mike looked concerned. "Not nice? Or worse?"

"Worse," Alison whispered.

"Let me see it."

Alison handed it over.

" 'Dear Alison Blake,' " Mike read. " 'I watch you on *Sticks and Stones,* and I have the feeling that you know I'm watching you. To me, you are like a perfect girl, and I'm sure you need someone to take care of you. I am that person. I hope you're not dating anyone or anything because I'd hate to have to move some jerk out of the way, but I'll do that if I have to. You and I are meant to be together. We will be. Promise.' " Mike looked up at Alison. "It's not signed."

"It gives me the creeps," Alison said, with a nervous laugh.

"Maybe we ought to do something about this."

"Like what?"

"I don't know. Tell the producers maybe."

"No way. Randy's not too thrilled with me already. I don't want to cause more trouble."

"Then we could tell Kate. She'd be sympathetic."

Alison shook her head. "There's nothing really threatening in this letter. Besides, stuff like this must happen all the time."

"Stuff like what?" Jamie sat down beside them.

Alison wanted to forget the letter, but Jamie was sitting there expectantly. "Just a creepy piece of fan mail."

"Well, let me see it," Jamie said, tugging it out of Alison's hand. "Oh wow." Jamie threw it down on the table. "Weirdsville."

"Mike thinks I should give it to someone."

"Don't bother. Stars get stuff like this all the time. One girl on *The Happydale Girls* used to have a regular pen pal. He wrote her the same thing every week."

"Which was?" Mike asked curiously.

"Just one line. 'I want to kiss your shoulder.' "

Alison and Mike broke into laughter.

"That was it?" Alison asked, relaxing a little.

Jamie nodded. "For months. Just a kiss on her shoulder."

Alison turned to Mike. "See, we're just getting excited because this is the first time I've gotten something like this, but it's not that strange."

"I guess," Mike said, going back to his lunch. "But I still don't like it."

"It comes with the territory," Jamie assured him.

"Aren't you having lunch?" Alison asked.

"I already grabbed a bite," Jamie lied.

Alison looked down at the hamburger. "I think Randy Ellis has taken away my appetite.

"Mine, too," Jamie agreed, with a grim smile. Ironically, it was getting easier not to eat because Randy had put a big, fat knot in her stomach.

"So what do you think of Shana Ellis?" Mike asked, changing the subject.

"She's sure got a pretty good role," Jamie noted.

"What do you think of her acting?" Alison asked.

"Average," Jamie said. And boy, did that bug her. She was just getting over Alison obtaining her role with no acting experience. Now she had to put up with a so-called actress whose main credential was her family tree.

"Don't let that attitude show," Mike warned. "We don't want to get on the wrong side of another Ellis."

After lunch, the trio headed back to the studio for the rest of the run-through. Mike had to stop in the costume department, leaving Alison and Jamie to walk back to their soundstage through a deserted part of the lot, where old, massive props sat like dinosaurs in the sun. Suddenly, Alison grabbed Jamie's arm.

Jamie stared at her. "What is it?"

"I just got the weirdest feeling. Like someone was following us." She turned and glanced over her shoulder. The sidewalk was empty.

"Hey, are you letting that fan letter freak you out?"

"I . . ."

"Look, if you're safe anywhere, you're safe here," Jamie said. "Calm yourself."

"You're right." Alison laughed shakily. "I'm just being silly."

Shana was already sitting at the table, looking over the script, when the girls arrived. "Hi," she greeted them. "Ready for part two?"

"*We* are," Jamie responded curtly.

Shana may have only been an average actress, but she wasn't stupid. "Hey, I'm a professional actress, too. I didn't get this part just because I'm Randy's niece."

"Really? You auditioned like anyone else?"

Shana reddened a little but didn't say anything.

"That's what I thought," Jamie said, turning away and taking her seat at the far end of the table.

"I hear you didn't have any experience when you got your part," Shana said, turning to Alison.

"But she did try out," Mike answered for Alison as he joined them at the table. "She's Jane because Dan thought she was terrific."

"I've been in a couple of movies," Shana said defensively. "I've gotten work on my own."

Alison looked at Shana's tight expression and felt sorry for her. If anyone knew what it was like to have people wondering if you were good enough, it was Alison. It didn't seem fair to hold Shana responsible for all the gripes the cast and crew had against Randy.

She leaned over to Shana and whispered, "Just do the job, and everything will be okay."

Shana looked at her gratefully. "I hope so. Thanks."

The rest of the run-through went a little better than the morning session. The cast relaxed more and brought out some of the script's humor. Randy held his sarcasm to a minimum.

That's why it was such a surprise when he got up after the run-through and said, "Mike, Alison, I want to see you in my office."

Mike and Alison looked at each other nervously. As she gathered her things, Jamie came over and said, "Do you have any idea why he wants to see you?"

"Not a one," Alison replied.

"Well, I'm sure it's nothing."

"I guess we'll find out," Alison said.

"Call me later."

Alison nodded and walked over to join Mike.

"You were great today," Mike said emphatically as they headed over to Randy's office.

"Not really," Alison shook her head.

"He'd better not mess with you," Mike said.

"Mike," Alison said with alarm, "don't start up with Randy."

"We'll see," Mike said grimly.

Randy was on the phone when Alison and Mike arrived in his office. He motioned them to sit down. "Ben, you're supposed to be the publicist. That means getting us good publicity, not this crap about unrest on the set." He hung up the phone and pushed aside a newspaper he had in front of him.

"I don't know where the columnists get these things, do you?" he asked, putting his feet up on his desk. He didn't wait for an answer. "I'd hate to hear that any of my stars were complaining to the press."

Is that why he called us here? Alison wondered wildly. *Does he think we're spreading rumors in the newspaper?*

But Randy had something else on his mind. "Now, what's all this about you two dating?"

Without thinking, a shocked Alison said, "How did you know?"

"So it's true," Randy replied with some satisfaction.

"I don't know that it's any of your business," Mike said, trying to keep his tone even.

Randy's laugh was sharp and harsh. "Hey, kid, everything that happens on my show is my business."

"We've only had one date," Alison said, hoping to pacify him.

"That's good. Then you won't miss each other much."

"What's the deal?" Mike demanded. "What do you care if we see each other?"

"Because it's not good for *Sticks and Stones.*"

"Why not?" Alison wanted to know.

Randy ticked off the reasons on his fingers. "I need you two, especially Mike, as a sex symbol, so I don't want him tied down to any one girl. Second, if he has to date someone, I don't want it to be the girl who plays his sister. And third, if it all goes bad for you two, the show can't waste time picking up the pieces. It's been my experience that these workplace romances never work out."

Alison clenched and unclenched her hands. Randy was talking as if her feelings for Mike were some sort of a bad business deal. It was humiliating.

"How did you find out about us?" Mike asked, stony faced.

"Someone saw you at the movies in Westwood."

"And ratted on us," Mike finished for him.

Randy shrugged. "Look, if it was only your first date like Alison says, this isn't a great romance yet. I just want to make sure it stays that way."

"Let me get this straight," Mike said. "Can we go to lunch? Maybe go shopping on a Saturday afternoon? What about a movie if it's the early, early show."

"Funny, Mike, but you're a smart kid. I'm sure I don't have to draw a picture for you."

Shaking, Alison had to lean against the wall the moment they were finally out of the office. "That was awful," she moaned.

"It wasn't good."

"He made us sound so . . . cheap."

"He doesn't know a damn thing about us. And he can't stop us from doing whatever we feel like," Mike declared.

Alison looked at him with surprise. "You mean you're going to ignore him?"

Mike grabbed Alison's hand. "*We* are."

Chapter 6

"Whew!" Jamie sat up and wiped the beads of perspiration from her forehead. *One hundred sit-ups. Pretty good.*

Jamic didn't know where she got the energy to do all those sit-ups, but lately she felt almost compelled to exercise. She wasn't eating much, but she was eating *something* after all, so those calories had to be worked off.

Just as she did after every workout, Jamie headed to the bathroom to check her weight. She probably got on the scale five or six times a day. She knew she couldn't lose much in the course of a day, but it made her feel good to check out the numbers.

At least she felt that way for a moment or two. But it seemed her good feelings never lasted long, maybe because she'd turn, catch a glimpse of herself in the full-length mirror, and realize she still didn't like what she saw. True, the numbers that registered on the scale told her that she had reached her target weight, even gone under it, but she didn't feel the way she thought she would when she finally reached her goal. If anything, she still felt a little heavy. No, Jamie told herself, with exercise and her current diet, she could knock off a few more pounds. Just thinking about it brightened her mood.

Jumping into the shower, Jamie wondered what she should wear on her date with David tonight. A real date. It was hard to believe they had gotten to this point.

But Jamie couldn't resist David's invitation. The way he asked her had been so cute. When she went out to wait for the studio car on Wednesday, there was a little yellow rubber ducky sitting on the stoop with a note tied around its neck, asking her for a date on Saturday night. For a moment she just stood there, then she broke into laughter. David had popped out of the bushes and said, "So does that mean yes?"

"Yes. If you can behave yourself."

David pasted a choirboy smile on his face. "Cross my heart."

Now, she wondered, what should she wear? She didn't even know what they were doing.

Rifling through her closet, Jamie found a blue sundress. She put it on and added dangling silver earrings and a silver bracelet. Instead of wearing her hair in the usual French braid, she decided to let it hang loose. It made her feel slightly wild.

So Jamie was just in the mood to be daring when David escorted her to his car and said. "Hey, why don't you drive?"

"Me?" Jamie asked with surprise. "I don't know how."

"Do you have your permit?"

Jamie nodded. "I just haven't had time to take driving lessons."

"Well, what about one now?"

Jamie began smiling. "All right!" Quickly, she climbed in the driver's seat. "You're taking a chance, you know."

"Nah. I'm a great teacher." He handed over the keys. "Now start the motor."

Careening a little, Jamie made her way down the street. "Now, turn here."

"I'm supposed to put on my blinker, aren't I?" she asked with confusion. "Where is it?"

David leaned over and switched it on for her. "Now after you turn, stay in the right lane and just keep going."

Although driving was nerve-racking, it was exhilarating, too. Jamie also had to admit she felt her feelings for David softening. It was awfully nice of him to let her drive. "So where are we going?" Jamie asked as they sped along.

"My favorite Italian restaurant."

Jamie had hoped that since David was picking her up at eight, they might skip eating. "Gee," she said, trying to concentrate on the road, "I thought we'd go to a movie."

"Afterward we can. I'm starving."

Jamie tried to nod pleasantly.

The restaurant was on the water. It wasn't one of those hip, modern places. With its faded checked curtains and worn wooden tables it looked as if it had been around for years and years.

''The food's great here,'' David told her as the hostess seated them. ''None of that nouvelle crud. They have real food here.''

Jamie's stomach tightened at the thought. She decided that spaghetti would be the easiest. With all that sauce, it would be easy to push around her plate.

This was the first time she had faced a big dinner since New York. *There's nothing to be nervous about,* she told herself. *You just won't eat it.* But she couldn't deny how uncomfortable she felt.

''So tell me about your play,'' Jamie said after they ordered.

David looked pleased that Jamie was interested. ''It's going great.'' He told her about the other actors and the director, then said, ''We're opening in a month. Did I tell you the play is being done in modern dress?''

Jamie giggled. ''Shakespeare in blue jeans?''

''Something like that.''

''Doesn't sound all that hoity-toity to me.''

''It's innovative.''

''I suppose that's one word for it,'' Jamie said, trying to hide her distaste as the spaghetti was put down in front of her.

David ignored the dig. ''What about you? That Randy guy still on your case?''

''Everybody's. By the time we taped yesterday, we were all so tense, people were blowing their lines. That's never happened before.''

''You don't think your job's on the line, do you?''

''I don't know,'' Jamie admitted worriedly.

"Hey, if something happens with *Sticks and Stones,* you could get into some real acting. I'm sure you could get into the theater."

"Really, after working in such a lowly medium as sitcoms?" How could a simple plate of spaghetti make her so nervous? Jamie wondered. Maybe because she was torn between wanting to devour it and just pushing it off the table, out of her sight.

"I think you could get into a crowd scene," David joked.

Jamie took a tiny bite of her food. "I don't want to work in the theater. Don't you get it?"

David leaned over. "Jamie, I know this is a sore spot, but I honestly believe the way you hone your craft is by doing classic plays."

"So, I'm shallow because I think my job is fun? Because I appreciate the things, like money, that go with it?"

"I didn't say shallow . . ."

"No, you just make fun of what I do all day."

David looked weary. "Eat your dinner, Jamie. It's getting cold."

Jamie knew she was overreacting, but suddenly everything was coming down on her really hard. The pressure of the day, the need to watch what she ate, David's harping on television versus the theater.

Jamie pressed on, determined to make her point, "You know, Kate Morton is one of the best writers in the business."

"She's no—" David shut up.

"No what? No Shakespeare? Well, twenty million people are going to watch our show. How many do you think will see your play? A hundred?''

Finally, David snapped. ''I don't know how many, but the ones that show up will have a brain in their heads.''

''That's it!'' Jamie said, slapping the table. ''I want to go home.''

''What! I've barely touched my food.''

''I don't care.''

''Hey, you're not the star of this show.''

''So finish your stupid dinner,'' Jamie said. And she sat there, her hands crossed in front of her chest, not saying a word while David shoved food into his mouth. Then he asked for the check.

Looking upset, he finally asked, ''Do you really want to go home?''

She didn't. Jamie had calmed down a little, and she would have liked to forget their stupid fight, but it wasn't like her to give in so easily. So the stubborn part of her nodded and she said, ''Yes, take me home.''

Jamie was as quiet on the way home as she had been at dinner. A far cry from the fun she had driving over here. She thought that she would just get out of the car without a good-bye, but David wasn't going to let her go that easily.

As Jamie grabbed her purse, David took it out of her hand and pulled her toward him. ''What are you . . .'' she sputtered.

''Shut up,'' David said, and then kissed her.

Jamie felt a little weak when David finally let her go.

She was so confused. Was she still angry? Or did she want to stay in this car forever?

''Maybe you can stop being so silly now,'' David said softly.

''Me?'' Jamie squeaked.

''Okay, okay. We.''

''No, you said me.'' Jamie knew how she felt now—mad. ''You think I'm the one causing all the trouble, when it's your sarcastic comments that always start things off.''

David looked as if he was going to apologize, but before he could say anything, Jamie bounded out of the car. ''Thanks for the driving lesson,'' she called over her shoulder.

Jamie flew through the door and flung herself on the couch. Thank goodness she was alone tonight. Her mother and Elsie were having dinner at her dad's. *I'm just going to enjoy being here by myself. No questions, no answers.*

But after going over and over the disastrous events of the evening, Jamie began feeling alone and scared. How could she have screwed things up so badly? one little voice whispered in her ear. Another voice, a bit more loudly, told her everything was David's fault.

Depressed, she was staring at the ceiling when the phone rang.

''Hello,'' she answered dully.

''Jamie, it's Alison.''

''What's up?'' Alison had never called her on a Saturday night.

"Mike and I are over at my house, and Steve stopped by to pick up a CD. We're going to be hanging out for a while. I thought maybe you could join us."

Jamie could read between the lines. Alison was trying to play matchmaker. Well, maybe being with Steve and Alison and Mike was a good idea tonight. Anything beat being here alone.

"I'd like that."

"Do you need to get ready?" Alison asked.

Jamie laughed a not altogether amused laugh. "As a matter of fact, I'm all ready for a date."

"Well, good," Alison said uncertainly. "Steve's rarin' to come and pick you up."

"I'll be here." Jamie forced some gaiety into her voice.

She had to give Steve credit. He made it in record time. And it was a relief to spend the whole drive back to Alison's in light banter. Steve had taken a summer job at a men's clothing store in Westwood and regaled her with stories of the customers who came in, each in search of the perfect outfit.

"Hey, how come Mike's allowed at Alison's?" Jamie asked as they pulled into the driveway. "I thought her parents weren't very happy about their relationship."

"About as happy as Randy Ellis. But her parents went to a wedding in Palm Springs, so Alison's taking advantage."

Estelle, the housekeeper answered the door. "They're out by the pool," she said politely.

As happy as Jamie was with her new living accommodations, she really wished that she had a pool in her backyard. And what a glorious backyard it was, Jamie thought as she wandered down the stone walk surrounded by flowers and over to the pool area. The scent of lemon trees filled the air.

"Hey," Mike said as they approached. He was stretched out on one of the lounge chairs.

Alison was in the pool, swimming the length in long, even strokes.

"Ali said to tell you there're suits in the cabana if you want to swim," Mike informed them.

Jamie didn't feel like messing up her outfit. "Not for me."

"Maybe later," Steve said, pulling up a chair.

Alison popped out of the pool. "Hi, you guys," she said. "It didn't take you long to get here."

"Nothing takes very long in that car," Steve said.

"I had a driving lesson tonight," Jamie said without thinking.

"From who?" Alison asked conversationally.

Uh-oh, Jamie thought. She really didn't want to talk about David in front of Steve and the others. "Just a neighbor."

Alison climbed out of the pool and toweled herself off. "Boy, I wish I could find the time for some driving lessons. It seems like I've had my permit forever."

"What do you need to drive for?" Steve asked. "You've got that great limo to take you everywhere you want to go."

"Not everywhere," Jamie said, "mostly to work, but they do make exceptions, sometimes for personal things.

It'll be taking us to that boutique opening tomorrow,'' she added, making a face.

"It won't be so bad,'' Alison said.

"What do you do at a boutique opening?'' Steve asked.

"They just open the door and let the customers fall in,'' Mike joked.

"Very funny,'' Jamie said. She turned to Steve to explain. "You've heard of Carol Connor, the big designer?''

Steve nodded.

"She's opening a boutique on Rodeo Drive, mostly for kids our age. So, she's arranged with the publicity department at the studio for big teenage stars to be there. Big stars like us,'' she deadpanned.

"But what exactly do you do?'' Steve inquired.

"Sign autographs, mostly,'' Alison told him.

"Smile,'' Jamie said, making a horrible face.

Alison giggled, but she said, "I think it'll be fun meeting some fans.''

"Well, I hope the studio has made arrangements for security,'' Mike said forcefully.

"Oh, Mike, they don't even know I'm getting those stupid letters. Why would they beef up the security?''

"You've gotten more?'' Steve asked.

Alison pulled on a terry-cloth robe. She was suddenly feeling very cold. "Yeah, another one at the studio, and one at home.''

"Here!'' Mike exploded. "You didn't tell me.''

"It just came this afternoon,'' Alison said in a small voice. "I was trying to forget about it.

"I want to see it," Mike told her.

"All right. I left it in the study."

"Mike, this is getting serious," Jamie said quietly, once Alison had left the room. "It's one thing to get this stuff at the studio, but at the house? That means this creep knows where she lives."

"I know, I know."

"Maybe you should tell Randy," Jamie fretted.

"Like he would care," Mike said with disgust. "Do you know what he would do if he knew I was here?"

"It must be hard for you," Steve said sympathetically.

"Sure is. Alison's parents aren't thrilled about us see-ing each other, and Randy said no way."

"But you're sitting here anyway," Steve pointed out.

"Yeah. Alison and I will find a way."

Jamie picked at some lint on her dress. She was re-lieved to find out that she didn't feel any jealousy about Alison and Mike. Some things were just meant to be, and she supposed that Alison and Mike were one of those. Her mind drifted over to David. Had she made a mistake send-ing him away? *That kiss.* She had never felt anything like it before. But she and David couldn't even have a conver-sation without it degenerating into a fight. Who needed the aggravation? Her gaze focused on Steve. He was so sweet. He thought being on *Sticks and Stones* was great. *It will just be Steve from now on,* she told herself firmly. *I could do a lot worse.*

Alison came back on the patio clutching a piece of plain white paper. "Here it is," she said, handing it over to Mike.

" 'Dear Alison,' " he read, " 'I hope you got my last letter. Sometimes fan mail gets lost at the studio, so I decided to write you at your house, where I know you'll get this. But I'm not just another fan. I'm the man of your dreams. You'll find out. Very soon, I hope.' "

"This guy's bad news," Jamie responded.

"Look," Steve said seriously. "This guy sounds extremely weird. Don't you think you ought to tell someone?"

"I can take care of Alison," Mike said firmly.

"But shouldn't you at least tell Alison's parents?" Jamie asked.

"My father wasn't happy when I took this job," Alison reminded her. "He'd probably make me quit. Besides, you told me yourself, this kind of stupid stuff goes with the territory."

"I guess," Jamie replied uncertainly.

"Besides, he doesn't say anything really threatening," Alison continued. "Maybe he'll just fade away."

Alison's comment hung in the air. It was clear no one believed that would happen. Not even Alison.

Alison looked at herself in the mirror. Carol Connor had sent over one of her outfits to wear to the opening, and it was really hot.

Mrs. Blake walked into her room. "Lord, I wore something like that in the seventies. I can't believe bellbottoms are back."

Alison's cropped gauzy top, tied at the waist, matched

the bell-bottoms her mother was staring at. Her belly button peeked out between the shirt and the pants.

"I wish the shirt was longer, though," her mother commented.

"Oh, Mom," Alison groaned. "You mean you never showed a little bit of skin when you were young?"

Mrs. Blake had to laugh. "Maybe an inch or two."

"I'm glad you remember," Alison said tartly.

Trying to keep an easy tone, Mrs. Blake said, "Estelle said you had a small party last night."

"I would have told you myself, but I was sleeping when you got back this morning."

"Mike was there?"

"You said not to have him when I was home alone. I wasn't."

"Your father and I aren't going to forbid you to see Mike. We're not stupid. We know that would only make you want to date him more."

Why did parents always think they could use psychology on you? "Geez, Mom, it's not that he's some kind of delinquent. He's a wonderful person. You'd find that out if you got to know him a little better."

"Well, maybe we should have him over for dinner."

That sounded excruciating to Alison, but she knew her mother was making an effort.

"Yeah, that would be good." *Maybe she'll forget about it,* Alison thought.

Although the studio had told her that the boutique opening was a big deal, Alison wasn't prepared for the mob scene waiting at the store. The crowd was being kept behind ropes by the security people, but as Alison got out of the car and the kids saw her, they erupted.

Alison glanced over at them, and gave a wave and a smile. One blond young man in a T-shirt and jeans caught her eye. He wasn't calling her name, just staring at her. With a start, Alison wondered if he was the one who had been writing her. *Come on, Alison,* she told herself, *what makes you think he's the one?* But the fun of the crowd's excitement disappeared. Alison turned away and hurried into the store.

Jamie was already at the boutique, waiting in the designer's office. She also looked terrific, in a long, slim skirt and filmy blouse and a vest. With a shock, Alison realized how thin Jamie had become. The curves that had made Alison so jealous in the past were totally gone, and Jamie was able to pull off that slinky skirt without a hint of hips. But as Alison's gaze traveled up to Jamie's face, she realized that her co-star was also looking pretty haggard. Even her hair seemed to have lost its bounce.

Alison was about to make a concerned remark when Jamie grabbed her arm.

"Look who's here. I don't believe it!"

My pen pal! The sudden, irrational thought shot through Alison's brain, but to her relief, Jamie was pointing at Shana Ellis, also wearing a Carol Connor original.

"What's she doing here?" Alison hissed.

"I have no idea. No one mentioned she was coming, but Cindy's with her."

Cindy brought Shana over to them. Alison noted they

both looked embarrassed. "Hi," Cindy said. "We have an addition to our team."

"I didn't know we were going to be such a big team," Jamie said archly.

"Everyone thought that since Shana is new, this might be a good way to introduce her."

"Everyone? Or Randy?" Jamie asked.

"C'mon, Jamie, try and be professional here," Cindy said.

"No, wait a minute," Shana interrupted. "Let's be up-front here. I don't blame Jamie for being upset. And Alison, too, even if she's a little more polite about it."

"Okay, let's be up-front," Jamie said. "You're not one of the stars of this show, at least not yet. I guess your *uncle*"—Jamie emphasized the word—"has big plans for you."

"I don't know whether I should be here, either, but I am," Shana continued, ignoring Jamie's comment. "Maybe you two hate me or think I can't act my way out of a paper bag. But hate *me,* not Randy. And try to be honest about whether I have any talent."

Even Jamie didn't have a comeback for this direct approach.

"All right?" Shana insisted.

Jamie shrugged. "All right."

"Let's try to just get out there and do the job now," Alison said.

Cindy looked around. "Carol Connor is supposed to be here to greet you herself. I wonder where she is."

A woman hurried into the office, but it wasn't Carol.

This harried soul was obviously one of her assistants. In her arms was a big bouquet of flowers. "Alison?" she asked. "These are for you."

"Are they from Carol?" Alison asked with surprise, but the woman had disappeared.

"She wouldn't be sending just me flowers," Alison said as she tore open the tissue. "Oh, they're gorgeous!" she said, fumbling around for a card. But when she read it, it fluttered out of her hand.

Jamie picked it up and read, " 'Alison, I'm here watching you. I'll never let you out of my sight.' "

Chapter 7

Alison didn't know how she made it through the afternoon. She was as nervous as a cat.

She had made up her mind to tell Cindy about all the letters, but just as she was about to pull her aside, Carol Connor had swept into the room.

Wearing one of her own creations, a cloudlike dress in a heavenly blue, Carol beamed at all of them, obviously not noticing the fear on Alison's face nor the concern on Jamie's.

"The crowds have gathered, my dears," she informed them, patting her meringue-colored hair, twisted in a French roll. With a practiced eye, she looked them over. "You look wonderful in those outfits. Just what I had in mind when I designed them."

"What would you like the girls to do?" Cindy said in her most professional voice.

"In just a moment or two, I'll escort the girls out. I'll make a short speech welcoming everyone, and they can say hello. Then, they will move to the table we've set up for autographing.''

''I don't think I can do this,'' Alison moaned in a low voice to Jamie.

But before Jamie could say anything, two security men hustled Alison, Jamie, and Shana into the shop. There was a burst of confusion as the security people tried to maneuver them to the makeshift stage. Flashbulbs blinded the girls, and when there was a loud pop, Alison felt the shivers climb her back. It had sounded like a gun.

''It'll be all right. Nothing can happen here,'' Jamie assured her, as she practically pushed Alison onto the stage. ''There're security people everywhere.''

Alison nodded, but she wasn't comforted.

Carol Connor moved to center stage, subtly positioning the girls on either side of her. She leaned into the mike. ''Welcome, everyone. As you might guess, I'm delighted to finally open a store of my own, where the people who like my clothes can come and look at them, try them on, and hopefully buy them!''

The crowd laughed.

''Now, I'd like you introduce three special friends of mine from that great, new hit show, *Sticks and Stones*.''

Shana just waved and said hello, but Jamie stepped up to the mike. ''We're all happy to be here, and of course, we're happy to be wearing these terrific outfits.'' Jamie whirled around to the applause of the crowd.

Alison knew it was her turn to say something, so she stepped up to the mike. But it was going to be hard to say something loud enough to cover the beating of her heart.

She scanned the crowd. She hoped that it would be mostly girls. That way she could keep her eye on the guys. But in the sea of faces, there were plenty of guys, and they all seemed to be staring at her.

"I . . . I just want tell you, I think Carol's clothes are lovely, and I'm sure you will, too." Alison turned away from the microphone.

"Thank you, girls," Carol said smoothly. "They will be available for autographs, so meet the stars and buy, buy, buy," she said with a laugh.

The guards whisked the girls to the autograph table.

"Are you okay?" Jamie whispered.

"I think so."

They sat behind the table. The kids started to line up for autographs. Alison tried to be pleasant to the fans who came up to her, but instead of listening to their compliments, she scanned their faces, especially the male faces, wondering if there were ulterior motives lurking behind their smiles. When one guy with long hair and an earring started babbling about how pretty she was, Alison could feel her stomach muscles clench. Then a girl tapped him lightly on the arm and said, "You've got to forgive Jimmy, but he's totally nuts about you."

It seemed unlikely a stalker would have a girlfriend. Alison relaxed a little, but the experience unnerved her.

"Finally," Alison said, as the last of the fans were ushered out of the boutique. She felt a little weak.

Shana got up from her chair and came up to Alison and Jamie. "Wasn't that fun?" she said enthusiastically.

Alison just stared at her, but Jamie, realizing Shana

didn't know she was putting her foot in it, said, "Sure. The best."

"I hope you didn't think I was being a jerk earlier," she continued, "but I had to stand up for myself."

Jamie knew it would be easy to put Shana down, but the most important thing seemed to be getting Alison out of the boutique in one piece. "You're right, Shana. Things will work out. We'll see you at work tomorrow."

"I hope Shana didn't think we were just blowing her off," Alison said, as Jamie hustled her to the limo.

"Lord, Alison, here you are afraid to look over your own shoulder, and you're worried that poor Shana Ellis had her feelings hurt."

As soon as the door slammed, Alison leaned against the backseat and let out a rush of breath.

"Okay, that's it, Alison. Enough is enough. You need to call somebody in on this."

Alison nodded.

"Do you want to tell your folks first, or Randy?" Jamie asked.

"What a choice," Alison groaned. "I'll have to think about it. Ask Mike, maybe."

"I know he wants to take care of you himself," Jamie said sympathetically, "but even Mike will see you need some backup on this."

Mike didn't at first. Alison wished she didn't have to tell Mike over the phone about the flowers, but getting out to see him didn't seem worth the hassle it would cause with her parents. Whispering on the phone in her bedroom, Alison told Mike the whole story.

"I should have been there," Mike said, upset.

"Mike, Randy would have found out for sure if you were at the boutique. There were photographers everywhere."

"You think I care about that when you're in trouble?" Mike fumed.

"I almost told Cindy, but I guess it will be better to go right to the top and discuss it with Randy. Don't you think I should tell him tomorrow?"

"Yeah, I do. I guess going with you would just make things worse," Mike said with a sigh.

"It will be better if I do it myself."

As long as she was going to do it herself, Alison decided she'd better do it first thing in the morning, before her resolve got lost in the hustle-bustle of the day. Since her mother had a dental appointment near the studio, Alison decided to skip the limo and have Mrs. Blake drop her off early.

Perfect, she thought. *I can just slip in and see Randy and get this taken care of. I hope he's had his coffee.*

Randy's secretary wasn't in, so Alison timidly knocked on his office door.

"Yeah, come in," Randy called.

"Good morning," Alison said, plastering a smile on her face.

"What's up Alison?"

"Well, it's about a problem I've been having," she began.

Randy frowned. "It's a little early in the morning for problems, isn't it?"

So much for her hopes of catching Randy in a good mood. "It's not something that happened this morning. It's about some of the fan mail I've been receiving."

"The publicity department handles fan mail."

"Yes, but—"

The jangling of the phone interrupted Alison. Randy grabbed it.

"Yeah? Jay? What do you mean the ratings are down?" The stream of cuss words out of Randy's mouth must have burned Jay's ears. "This will be the first week we're not in the top ten." His voice rose even higher. "Well, I don't want to read about this in the columns. Bury this, you understand me?" Randy's voice rolled like a wave.

He slammed down the phone and focused on Alison as if he had forgotten she was there. "You didn't hear a thing. Got that?"

Alison nodded.

"I don't want any rumors flying around this studio. Now get out of here. I've got some real problems to deal with."

Alison practically ran out of the office. She bumped right into Shana.

"Alison, what's wrong?"

"Your uncle . . ." she cried.

Shana put her arm around Alison and led her off to the dressing room. "So what did he do?" Shana asked, once she had Alison settled in a chair with a glass of water.

Alison hated herself for crying, and she didn't especially want to confide to Shana about the letters. But with

Shana looking at her expectantly, Alison felt she had to say something.

"I've been getting these letters. . . ."

"What kind of letters?"

"Creepy. And those flowers I got yesterday? They were from him."

"Who is he?"

"They're always unsigned. I was going to ask Randy for help, but he was in such a bad mood, I never got to it."

"I'll talk to him," Shana offered.

"No. I really think I should do it. I just have to wait for the right moment."

"I don't know if you can afford to wait," Shana said doubtfully.

"I'll do it soon, I promise." Alison decided to confide a little more. "Before I got this part on *Sticks and Stones,* I was just this timid rabbit. I want to be able to handle things on my own, Shana."

"Okay, I get it, but don't wait too long."

Mike walked into the dressing room and looked from Alison to Shana. "You told her," he guessed.

"I had to."

"Did you talk to Randy?"

"He was busy," Alison said. She was afraid to tell Mike how rude Randy had been. He might go storming into Randy's office if she did. "I'll take care of it as soon as I can."

"Soon. Promise?"

"I will."

Mike gave Alison a pat on the shoulder, then he and

Shana went to pick up their scripts. Alison knew she should be looking over her script, but she felt like she didn't have enough energy to pick it up off the coffee table. She was just sitting, staring into space when Jamie arrived.

"What's wrong?" Jamie demanded.

Alison filled her in on the latest.

"Darn that Randy," Jamie said angrily. "I'm going to talk to him myself."

"No, Jamie, I've already told Mike and Shana I want to do this my own way."

"I won't say anything about the letters if you don't want me to, but I don't think any of us have to take his rudeness. I'm going to call him on it."

Before Alison could stop her, Jamie stormed out of the dressing room, her eyes blazing. She hated bullies, and Randy was king of the bullies.

She knocked briefly at Randy's door, then opened it without waiting for an answer.

"What do you want, Jamie? I seem to be having a lot of uninvited visitors this morning.

"That's what I want to talk to you about," Jamie blazed.

"Save it! But as long as you're here, I have something to say. Sit." He pointed to a chair."

Jamie, a little unnerved about this turn of events, sat. Nevertheless, she was ready to continue. "Randy, I think—"

"*I* think, you're beginning to look like a broom. A broom that's been worked a little too hard."

"What?"

"Are you on some ridiculous diet?" Randy continued. "You're skin and bones, and believe me it's beginning to show on camera. You didn't look like this in the early episodes."

Jamie could feel herself breaking out into a sweat. "I needed to lose a few pounds," she finally said.

"Well, you've lost them, and frankly, it hasn't done a thing for you. I want to have you weighed. Then I'm going to monitor you and make sure you're putting on at least three pounds a week. Got that?"

Three pounds a week? A horrible stuffed feeling came over Jamie. She was barely choking down a salad and some yogurt each day. She couldn't possibly eat enough to put on that much weight.

"I don't think I can," she said faintly.

Randy's laugh was harsh. "You'd better. Now would you mind leaving me alone. I've got work to do."

Jamie wandered out in a daze. She had totally forgotten about Alison and her reason for seeing Randy in the first place. All she could think about was all the awful food that Randy wanted her to stuff down herself. She wasn't kidding when she told him she couldn't start eating like that again. It was terrifying to think about putting on weight.

The assistant director was gathering everyone for the run-through. Listlessly, Jamie nodded and headed over there. Alison caught up with her, and put her hand on her shoulder. Catching a look at Jamie's face, Alison said, "You look like someone's after *you*."

"My stalker is named Randy."

"Oh, Jamie, I knew I shouldn't have let you go in there. He must have been furious that you blasted him."

"Blasted him? I didn't get that far."

"What happened?"

Jamie didn't want to tell her. She was sure that no one else had noticed her weight loss, other than to think how great she looked. She didn't want to put ideas into people's heads that she was having some sort of a stupid weight problem. "Nothing. He was just as rude to me as he was to you."

"What a jerk," Alison said. "But let's forget about it now. We can't screw up just because Randy's having a temper tantrum."

As the cast gathered around the table, Alison noticed how different the mood was from the way things used to be. Rodney, who played Jamie's little brother, used to always spout off, offering the cast bits of esoteric knowledge from his extensive reading. Now, he was subdued. Sliding into his seat, he opened his script and barely looked around at any of his castmates.

Donna and Ben, on the other hand, wore tight, hard expressions. Alison always found it amazing that Randy could be as curt with the two stars of the show as he was with the kids. Donna usually acted professional if cool, but several times, Ben had erupted, arguing with Randy about the direction he thought the show should take.

Kevin Voight, the director, tried to play peacemaker. Sometimes it worked; sometimes it didn't. The most unhappy person on the set seemed to be Kate Morton, and it was showing in her scripts. Randy was always saying that the shows weren't as funny as they were in the beginning, and now Alison had to agree with him. She was sure that Kate wasn't feeling very funny. More than anyone except Dan, Kate was responsible for the early success of the show. It had been her baby. Kate must feel like her baby had been kidnapped by a terrorist.

Kevin was about to begin the run-through, when Randy came up to the table where they were all sitting.

What now? Alison inwardly groaned.

But Randy seemed subdued for a change. "I just got a call from the network president. Those of you who read the trade papers may know that some of the network affili-ates are in town. As part of their tour, they'll be watching the taping of *Sticks and Stones*. There will be a party after-ward."

There was a slight buzz at this news. The network af-filiates were the stations that aired *Sticks and Stones* all over the country. It was a good sign that they were inter-ested in watching them tape.

"But," Randy continued, "there's some bad news that goes along with this. The only day the affiliates have free is Thursday, so that means we're going to have to tape a day early."

"Now wait a minute," Ben said, standing up. "It's the middle of Monday morning, and we haven't even looked over the script yet. Do you think we'll really be ready by Thursday?"

Randy shrugged. "You'll have to be."

"But without enough time, we can mess up," Donna

chimed in. "That's the last thing we want to do in front of affiliates."

Mike, sitting next to Alison, reached under the table and held her hand. She knew it was clammy, but she didn't care. It showed her that Mike was as upset about all this arguing as she was.

Randy was starting to get angry, but everyone could see him trying to keep a lid on his temper. "This is your show, gang. I can't get up there and act it for you. You know how important it is to make a good impression on these people. If you don't put on a good show—on Thursday as scheduled—we're all in trouble."

Chapter 8

"I wish we could go home," Alison said.

"Why?" Jamie asked with a yawn. "By the time we get there, we'll just have to turn around and come back." Jamie stretched out on the couch that took up most of their dressing room and closed her eyes.

"Don't do that." Alison leaned over and gave her a little shake. "If you fall asleep, you'll never wake up, and they'll be calling us for the last rehearsal any minute."

Jamie opened one eye. "I think they'll have to move me out there in a wagon."

"I know, I know," Alison said. "It has been exhausting."

Ever since Randy's announcement on Monday, the cast had been working double-time. Rehearsals ran longer, breaktimes and lunchtimes, shorter. Everyone was exhausted, and nerves were on edge. With all the pressure they were under, Alison hadn't had much time to think about any weird fans, and that, at least, had been a big relief. There hadn't been any more letters. Unfortunately, there had been two phone calls.

They had both come at home, early in the morning when Alison was getting ready to go to work. The first time, Alison hadn't thought anything of it. The line had seemed dead, but Alison had detected some breathing.

"Hello? Hello?" she'd said insistently.

When no one answered, Alison had hung up, figuring it was a wrong number. But it had happened the next day, again before she left for work, and that time the caller had whispered her name.

How had he gotten her phone number? Alison wondered. But whoever it was already had her address, and she supposed her phone number wouldn't be that hard to get. The Blakes had been listed in the directory until just a few months ago.

Alison mentioned the calls to Mike and Jamie, who sympathized, but with everyone so busy, their concern had gotten lost in the everlasting nitty-gritty of trying to finish the show on time and in good order.

Alison sipped at the tea that one of the production people had brought her. "Have you thought about this affiliates party at all? Donna said we should have escorts."

Jamie sat up. "I know. I took five seconds and called Steve. He was all excited about going with me."

"Steve? Not David."

"I told you. I'm through with David. What about you?"

"I'm not going with anybody if I can't go with Mike," Alison said determinedly.

"But you know Randy will go crazy if you two show up together."

"So we'll each come alone. It's stupid to pretend we're dating other people when we don't want to."

"If that's what you want."

Alison looked at Jamie. She noticed that Jamie hadn't eaten any of the sandwiches that had been brought in for them. Clearly, Jamie was on some sort of a diet, which wasn't doing her any good, as far as Alison could see. She remembered noticing Jamie's strange eating habits even in New York. Mike and Donna had commented to Alison about it. Rodney had told Jamie she looked like she had the flu, but Jamie had just brushed it off and said she was fine.

Now that she was feeling closer to Jamie, Alison wanted to have a serious talk with her about dieting, but a good moment never seemed to come. Maybe, though, now was the time.

"Jamie," Alison began, "I'm beginning to worry about you. You never seem to eat anything."

Jamie snapped to attention.

"You haven't been eating much for a long time," Alison continued, feeling her way into this touchy topic.

Oh, not you, too, Jamie thought. She was glad she hadn't told Alison about her conversation with Randy. It would just cause Alison to nag her even more.

Before Alison could probe further, Shana walked into their room.

"Time to go back?" Jamie asked. Tired as she was, she'd rather be onstage than answering questions about her eating habits.

Shana shook her head. "Not quite yet. But I need a favor. Maybe one of you can help me."

Alison and Jamie looked at her expectantly.

"It's sort of embarrassing, but I don't know anyone I'd want to invite to this party."

"I'm not going with anyone," Alison said. *At least not anyone you can know about,* Alison added to herself.

"Really?" Shana asked with surprise. "I thought everyone was supposed to have a date."

Alison just shrugged.

"So you don't have a date?" Jamie asked, a plan forming in her mind.

"No. I'm between boyfriends at the moment, and none of my friends really fills the escort bill. The guys I know barely own a shirt, much less a tie. Do you know *anyone?*" Shana pleaded.

Alison shook her head. "I've really lost touch with most of my high-school friends. All except Steve, and he's taking Jamie."

"I might know someone," said Jamie.

"Who?" Shana asked eagerly.

"An actor. His name is David." Jamie could feel Alison staring at her with surprise. "I'll give him a call."

"Oh, would you?" Shana asked gratefully.

"I'll do it before I go home."

Shana turned to Alison. "Have you gotten any more letters?"

Alison shook her head, but Jamie did say, "A few suspicious calls now."

"Randy was out of town yesterday, and I haven't had a chance to speak to him today, but I will."

"Don't worry about it. We're all so busy now. Let's get this taping and party over, and then we can worry about it." Alison hoped she sounded braver than she actually felt.

Shana had barely closed the door behind her when Alison turned to Jamie and said, "I can't believe you're going to fix her up with David."

"Why not?"

"What if he likes her?"

"So? I told you I'm dating Steve now."

Alison gave her an unbelieving look.

"David is too much trouble," Jamie said, fussing with her teacup. "I told you that."

"Hmm?" was all Alison would say.

Jamie wasn't quite sure why she was going to all the trouble of fixing David up with Shana. Maybe she wanted to prove to herself—and David—that she didn't care about him. Cared about him so little that she would happily have him date somebody else. She also tried to convince herself it was a nice gesture to fix up two friends. Also, it gave her an excuse to call him.

But she couldn't deny the pang she felt when David quickly agreed to go with Shana. "Sounds like fun," he said.

"You'll be around a lot of television people," Jamie said a little sarcastically.

"Hey, just because I don't want to read their lines, doesn't mean I don't want to eat their food."

"I'm going with Steve," Jamie told him, even though he hadn't asked.

"That's nice," David said pleasantly. "I'll see you there."

Jamie had expected to get a lift out of arranging a date for David, proving to both of them she wasn't serious about their own relationship, but when she hung up the phone, she felt hurt and sad. She was even more down when Shana thanked her for fixing the whole thing up. Shana was pretty cute, Jamie realized. Was she David's type?

Now Jamie felt discouraged. As well as tired and hungry. She could barely drag herself onstage for the evening's last rehearsal. At least Randy wasn't around.

Jamie knew she was feeling so lightheaded that she wasn't saying her lines properly, but she didn't expect the wave of blackness that swept over her during the middle of the rehearsal. The last thing she remembered was trying to figure out what she was supposed to say.

When Jamie finally opened her eyes, she was on the floor surrounded by a concerned cast and crew.

"What happened?" she asked woozily.

"You fainted," Kate Morton informed her. "I've called the studio doctor."

"No, I don't need him," Jamie said, trying to rise. "I feel fine."

"Forget about it," Mike said. He lifted her in his arms and carried her to the couch on the set. "Just rest here."

"But you've got to rehearse here," Jamie said, getting

more upset by the second. Not only had she screwed up by fainting, she had stopped the rehearsal dead in its tracks.

"Rehearsal is over," Kevin Voight declared. "We're all exhausted, obviously. I think the best thing to do is go home and get some sleep."

"But Randy . . ." one of the production assistants protested.

"I'll talk to Randy when he gets back from dinner," Kevin said firmly. "Now everyone go home except Jamie. I'll wait with her for the doctor."

"I'll wait too," Kate said.

Jamie could see that she was stuck. Kevin wasn't about to let her just go home and rest. She closed her eyes. Usually, she would have raised hell. Too bad she just didn't have the energy for it.

By the time the doctor arrived, most of the cast had followed Kevin's edict and gone home. Alison had asked if there was anything she could do, but Jamie just shook her head.

"Hello, Dr. Wright," Kate said, bringing the small, middle-aged man over to the couch. "Here's our patient."

Jamie was glad that Kate had stayed. She was one of Jamie's favorite people on the set, and it made her feel good to see Kate showing such concern.

The doctor smiled at her as he took her pulse. "So how are you feeling?"

"Tired," Jamie said, as he continued examining her.

"Could you excuse us, please?" Dr. Wright said pleasantly to Kate and Kevin. As soon as they were gone, he turned to Jamie. "When was the last time you ate?"

"Earlier," Jamie said vaguely.

"I don't think so," Dr. Wright said firmly. "Unless by 'earlier' you mean last week sometime. I can see that you haven't been eating properly. You're skin and bones, and it's beginning to affect your health," he said bluntly.

Jamie was too tired to deny any of it.

"I've seen other young actresses diet themselves into sickness, and we have to make sure that doesn't happen to you. Right now you need rest and nourishment. If I can't count on you to get both, you will have to be hospitalized."

That made Jamie sit up and take notice. "No, please."

"Then you know what you have to do."

Jamie nodded. She'd rest anyway, and she'd eat a little more than usual, but that was it.

"Fine. Then have someone drive you home, and I'll make an appointment to see you in a couple of days."

"Why?" Jamie protested. "I'll be okay."

"I'll be the judge of that."

Jamie closed her eyes. Now Randy *and* this Dr. Wright would be watching her. How could she ever get them off her back?

"Boy, that was amazing," Alison said to Donna Wheeler as they walked offstage. "I thought the taping would be a disaster, but it went all right."

Donna patted Alison on the shoulder. "That's what makes us professionals, kiddo. When it looks like the whole thing's going to fall apart, we reach down inside and come up with a little bit extra.''

Alison glowed at Donna's description of her as a professional. She had been the novice for so long. Maybe she really was being accepted by the cast as one of them. ''Thanks.''

''It's true.'' Donna glanced over at Jamie. ''Even our fainting friend managed to come up with the right stuff.''

''I'm worried about her,'' Alison said.

''We all are,'' Donna said, lowering her voice. ''It's obvious that Jamie has been on some sort of extreme diet, and we've all tried to ignore it. We can't do that anymore.''

Alison sighed. ''The last thing I feel like is going to a party.''

''Me, too,'' Donna agreed. ''But hey, remember what I just said. We're actresses. We go and pretend we're having a good time.''

''That may be the hardest acting job I've done in weeks.''

By the time Alison got back to her dressing room, Jamie had already begun to change. Donna was right. It was time to help Jamie. But what could she do?

Jamie slipped a gold lamé dress over her head. Short, with a scooped neck, it was a gorgeous dress, but Alison noticed that without sleeves, the dress highlighted Jamie's very thin arms.

''Can I ride over to the party with you?'' Jamie asked. ''Steve's going to meet me there.''

''Sure,'' Alison said enthusiastically. ''If we both walk in together, it will look like neither of us has dates.''

Jamie smiled wanly. "We'll fool that idiot Randy."

"Jamie, what did the doctor say last night?" Alison asked seriously. "You mumbled something about being worn out when I asked you earlier."

"He wants me to get more rest. Eat more veggies. Say, didn't you think the taping went well? The bigwigs seemed to be laughing pretty hard."

Alison nodded, but she was thinking, *Okay, Jamie O'Leary, change the subject if you want, but you haven't heard the end of this.*

The party was being held at a new, high-tech nightclub called Verdi. The publicity department had alerted the press, and there were plenty of photographers waiting to take the stars' pictures as they walked in.

The party was already in full swing. A loud band played near the dance floor, which was made of a shiny metal. The walls were painted a slick silver, and steel sculptures stood strategically in corners. The cast of the hospital drama *Code Blue* were there too, along with P.R. people, newspaper and magazine columnists, and an assortment of other celebrities. It was the kind of party Jamie had always read about in *People* or *The Enquirer* and had drooled over. Now she was right here in the middle of it, all the noise, the craziness, the stars.

The cast of *Sticks and Stones* had been told to mingle especially with the people from the affiliate stations who had been at the taping, but Alison thought there was something to do that was more important.

"Let's get something to eat," Alison said determinedly, steering Jamie over to the buffet.

Jamie knew better than to say she wasn't hungry. She dutifully went to the lavish buffet table and filled her plate with food. "I think we'd better circulate now," Jamie told Alison. Mixing would also allow her to get away from Alison's prying eyes. Alison looked as though she knew just what Jamie was thinking, but they split up anyway and spent some time chatting up the various affiliates.

Jamie tried to eat, but her plate was still almost untouched when Steve tapped her on the shoulder. "Hi there."

"Hello. You look nice," she said approvingly, putting the plate on a table.

Steve patted the lapels of his new suit. "It helps to work in a men's clothing store."

Jamie's eyes roamed the room. Finally, she found who she was looking for. "Maybe we should go say hello to David and Shana."

Steve frowned. "I don't care if I never see David again."

"But I fixed them up," Jamie protested. "It's only polite to go over and see how they're doing."

"All right," Steve muttered, as he followed her across the room. "But I wouldn't have minded eating something first."

Jamie was pleased to note that David and Shana seemed to be barely talking. They were making a big production out of shoving hors d'oeuvres in their mouths and sipping at their drinks.

"Well, hi, you two," Jamie said, forcing herself to sound gay.

Both David and Shana looked up at her as if they were drowning and she was a life preserver.

"Hey, Jamie and Steve," David said, sticking out his hand for Steve to shake.

Jamie made the introductions. "So what do you think of this party?" Jamie asked conversationally.

"Good grub," David said swallowing a bite.

"Too much fish. I hate caviar," Shana said.

"Me, too," Steve agreed with a laugh. "Can you believe people are willing shove fish eggs down their throats?"

"Yeah, I can," David said, having another cracker with caviar.

"This party stuff is okay," Shana said, ignoring David, "but I'd rather be at a Dodgers game."

"You're a Dodgers fan?" Steve asked.

"The biggest."

"Uh-uh. I'm the biggest."

Without missing a beat, Steve and Shana launched into a discussion of the Dodgers—who was playing well, who wasn't, what the team's chances were of winning the pennant. David and Jamie just stood there feeling like a couple of fifth wheels.

While Steve and Shana chattered away, David whispered out of the corner of his mouth, "I hate baseball."

Jamie looked at him in surprise. "I remember. You

couldn't have cared less about the Dodgers that night at my house.''

"But I love the Lakers."

"Me, too." It just slipped out. Jamie didn't mean to sound so agreeable, but she did adore basketball.

"How come we never talked about the Lakers before?" David asked.

"I think we were too busy fighting." Jamie turned back to Steve, but he and Shana were heavy into a conversation about what seemed to be another of their great passions, the Beatles.

"How did they get from the Dodgers to the Beatles?" Jamie asked.

David made a face. "The Beatles are old hat. Now the Seattle sound, that's music."

Jamie nodded.

"Say, do you want to dance?"

Jamie looked at Steve. It was pretty clear he wouldn't notice if she disappeared into the dance-floor bustle.

"Why not?"

David smiled at her and led her out to the floor.

Alison, who was standing off in a corner with Mike, noticed David and Jamie dancing. "It looks like Jamie and David have found each other again."

"I wonder what happened to Steve?" Mike asked.

Alison looked around the room and pointed to where Steve and Shana were talking, looking as if no one else was in the room. "Steve seems occupied."

"Very."

Alison shook her head. "I guess you just never know."

"I know," Mike said, surreptitiously squeezing her hand.

"There's Cindy," Alison said, pulling her hand away. "She's coming over here."

"Alison, your dad's on the phone," Cindy told her.

"My father?" Alison asked in surprise.

"He says he needs to ask you something."

"Where's the phone?"

"You know where the coatroom is? Turn left, and there's a hallway that leads to the manager's office. It's in there."

"Okay, I'll be right back."

What could my dad want? Alison wondered as she pushed past laughing partygoers and went to get the call. It had to be something important for him to call her here.

The hallway was dark and quiet, very different from the noisy party that was going on just a few yards away. Gingerly, she made her way down the hall, past a few other doors, squinting to see a nameplate.

Suddenly, horribly, she felt an arm around her waist and a hand being clapped over her mouth. She couldn't breathe—could barely think. Kicking and struggling she tried to get away from her captor, but he was much bigger and stronger than she was. Then the dim light of the hallway turned into total darkness. Alison was thrown into a small, dank space. Terrified, she heard a door slam behind her.

Chapter 9

Alison listened to her own beating heart. For a moment anyway. Then she started screaming and pounding on the door.

Would anyone hear her? The band was so noisy. Alison was sure her shouts would go unnoticed.

And what if he comes back? Of course, he'll come back, a voice whispered inside her. *He wouldn't have thrown you in this closet if he wasn't going to come back.*

The fear that surged through Alison welled up and dissolved into more screams and pounding. She hardly noticed that her fists were becoming sore and bruised.

It seemed to Alison that she had been in the closet forever. The walls of the small enclosure began closing in, and Alison couldn't catch her breath. Maybe he wasn't coming for her. Maybe she was just going to die in here.

Weakly, she pounded again, and this time she heard the most wonderful sound in the world—Mike's voice.

"Ali! Are you in there?"

"Yes, yes!" she cried. "Get me out!"

"I'll find someone."

"Don't leave me," she begged.

"Just for a few seconds, hon. Hold on."

Alison began crying, but she tried to keep herself together. "Just a few seconds. He'll be right back," she said over and over.

Soon, she heard several voices, one of them Mike's. "Hold on," he said, "the manager is here. He's got a crowbar. You'll be right out."

A horrible noise began, and almost immediately, Alison could see light coming through the cracks in the wood. Finally, the door swung open, and Alison fell out into Mike's arms.

"Are you all right?" he demanded.

Alison nodded, brushing away tears.

"I'm Kurt Sanders, the manager of Verdi," a tall, concerned man said. "How did you get in there?"

"A man pushed me in."

Kurt Sanders turned to Mike. "Do you think we should call the police?"

"I sure do," Mike said emphatically.

Mr. Sanders looked worried. "On second thought, I'm not sure the network would appreciate that."

"The hell with the network!"

"Well, maybe I should check with someone."

Alison stood shaking next to Mike, who had his arm around her. "Can't we call the police from home? I want to go home," she said with a sob.

"Okay," Mike comforted her, "soon."

"Please, Mike."

"What should I do about the police?" Mr. Sanders asked.

"Check with your bigwigs. Make sure they know why we left. I'm taking Alison home." He pushed past Mr. Sanders and hustled Alison outside. The limo that had brought them was waiting, and Mike directed the driver to Alison's home.

Alison knew she should tell Mike exactly what happened, so if the police were called she could remember all the details, but all she seemed to be able to do was cry out her fear. Mike's arm around her felt warm and reassuring.

When they pulled into her driveway, Alison sat up and wiped her eyes. "My parents are going to be scared to death if they see me like this."

"Alison, we have to tell them the truth. This has gone on too long."

"But—"

"No buts. I'll handle everything."

Mrs. Blake paled when she opened the door to let Alison and Mike in. "What happened!"

"I'm all right, Mom."

Mr. Blake came into the hall. "Alison . . ."

"We'll explain everything," Mike said. "Let's go into the living room and sit down."

"Mike's right," Mrs. Blake said, giving her daughter a hug. "Let's go into the living room."

Mr. Blake was glaring at Mike as though this was his fault.

Alison caught the look and cried, "Mike saved me, Dad."

Mr. Blake immediately looked contrite. "It's all right, darling. But saved you from what?"

As soon as they were settled, Mike said, "Alison has been getting threatening letters and calls from a crazy fan. Then, at the party, someone pushed her into a service closet and locked the door."

Mr. and Mrs. Blake seemed horrified. "Are you all right?" her mother asked, taking her daughter's face in her hands.

"Why didn't you tell us about these threats, Ali?" Mr. Blake demanded.

Alison felt the tears come to her eyes. "I was afraid you'd make me quit the show."

Mrs. Blake kissed her daughter's hair. "Let's not even think about that right now. Did you tell anyone at the show?"

"I tried, but . . ." Alison faltered. She had never even told her parents how difficult life at *Sticks and Stones* had become with Randy Ellis running the show. She had been so determined to handle things herself.

"I think we better start at the beginning," Mike said. Quickly, he filled the Blakes in on Randy's dictatorial regime. "So when all this started," Mike finished, "Alison tried to tell Randy about it, but he flew off the handle about something else, and she just left his office."

"Great," Mr. Blake fumed. "My daughter's in danger, and she can't even go to her producer for help."

"I'm sorry you didn't think you could come to us, either," Mrs. Blake murmured.

"I didn't know how serious it was," Alison said.

"We made some mistakes," Mike admitted.

"At least you realize that," Mr. Blake said. "How did you know to follow Alison?"

"I was worried. When Cindy said she had gotten a phone call, it didn't register for a minute, then I realized it might be that guy again. I didn't think he'd go this far, though."

"How did he get into the party?" Mr. Blake wanted to know. "Wasn't there any security?"

"There were guards," Mike said. "And I think they were checking names at the door, although they must have recognized me and Alison and Jamie because we just walked in."

Mr. Blake stood up. Alison had only seen him like this a few times in her life, but she remembered them well. It was her father blazing with fury underneath, but covering it with a cool facade.

"I'm going to call Randy Ellis at Verdi right now."

"Dad, do it tomorrow," Alison begged. "You can't interrupt the party."

"The hell I can't," Mr. Blake said through gritted teeth, and he headed toward the phone.

"He's going to make everything worse," Alison said, feeling more tears coming to her eyes.

"No, he isn't, Alison," Mike said. "Randy will have to listen your dad, and maybe we can get to the bottom of this."

"Thanks, Mike," Mrs. Blake said gratefully. "I agree." She turned to Alison. "I want you to go upstairs and take a bath. I'll make you a cup of tea. That'll make you feel better, don't you think?"

Alison was too tired to think. "I guess. But first, I want to hear what Dad told Randy Ellis."

They waited in silence until he returned. "I just gave your producer an earful," Mr. Blake said, coming back to the couch. "He agreed that there should be a police report filed."

"Tonight?" Alison asked with alarm.

"No, no, it can wait until tomorrow," her father said soothingly.

"Then I'm going to take Alison upstairs." Mrs. Blake helped her daughter rise.

"Wait, Clare. Before you and Ali go up, I'm going to say something, and I want to make sure that Alison hears it."

He turned to Mike and stuck out his hand. "I want to thank you. I know that something terrible could have happened to Alison tonight if you weren't watching out for her."

Mike shook his hand. "That means a lot to me."

"You're welcome here any time, Mike," Mrs. Blake added.

Alison gave him a hug and whispered, "Some good came out of this."

Once Alison had her bath, she slipped on her pajamas and got into bed. Her mother and father came up to say good night.

"Don't worry, Ali," her father said, "You're safe now."

But am I, Alison thought. *That crazy person is still out there. And he really is after me."*

Jamie looked at the clock: 9 A.M. She couldn't remember the last time she had slept so late on a Friday, but since the cast had taped a day early, they had been given today off.

She stared at the ceiling and thought about last night. It certainly hadn't turned out the way she expected.

First there had been that business with Alison. Jamie still wasn't sure what had happened. One minute Alison and Mike had been there, the next, they had just disappeared.

Jamie hadn't really thought much about it until rumors started sweeping the room. Someone had attacked Alison. Immediately, Jamie thought about that awful mail and wondered if she should say something. But what? And to whom?

Finally, she pulled Shana aside, though it wasn't easy getting her away from Steve.

"Did you hear about Alison?"

"Just that she got sick and had to go home."

"No, I think that guy got to her. The one that was writing the letters."

Shana's eyes widened. "Is she all right?"

"I don't know. Everyone seems to have a different story. Can you ask Randy what's going on?"

Shana nodded. "Let me see what I can find out."

While Shana was gone, Jamie sidled over to Steve. "You seem to be having a nice time."

Steve didn't catch the edge in her voice. "This is great! Isn't Shana terrific?"

"Oh, just swell."

"Where did she go?" Steve asked, looking around, a little like a lovesick puppy, Jamie thought.

"She had to ask her uncle something."

"Oh. Well, would you like to dance?"

Jamie looked over in David's direction. He was off getting some food at the buffet. "Okay."

Steve was usually so sensitive to people's feelings, but he didn't realize he might be hurting Jamie's feelings by chattering about Shana throughout the dance.

Actually, Jamie's feelings weren't really hurt much at all. It was pretty clear that Shana and Steve were made for each other, from their feelings about the Dodgers to their shared love of bowling, which Steve was rhapsodizing about at the moment.

"Bowling?" Jamie asked in surprise. "I thought bowling was only for nerds."

"Bowling is a lot of fun," Steve said indignantly.

"Right." Jamie made her decision. Let Steve and Shana bowl their way into the sunset. Jamie had to face facts. She looked over at David. He was really the one she wanted. The sparks flew between them, and sometimes those sparks set off fighting, but some of those sparks set off passion as well. In her heart, Jamie knew she hadn't really given David much of a chance. And she knew that she wanted to.

Just as the music was ending, Shana came over to them. "So?" Jamie asked.

"Randy was too busy too talk to me. He just shooed me away. But I sort of eavesdropped, and you were right, someone did get to Alison. He locked her in a closet."

"Is she all right?" Steve asked with concern.

"I think Mike took her home."

That was all Jamie had learned last night. Jamie got out of bed. Should she call Alison? She wanted to, but she didn't want to disturb her. Maybe later this morning.

Throwing on some clothes, Jamie went out into the kitchen. No one was home. A note on the kitchen table explained that her mother and Elsie had gone grocery shopping and would be home soon. Jamie decided she would try to eat breakfast. She had an appointment with the doctor on Monday, and she had the feeling that he wasn't kidding. Determinedly, she toasted a bagel and poured herself a glass of milk. It was a start.

But sitting down at the kitchen table, Jamie just stared at her food. It was strange. Almost as if she had forgotten how to eat. The same little voice that had been whispering in her ear lately said, *You're in trouble, girl.*

I am in trouble, she thought, frightened. But she didn't have a clue as to what she should do about it.

Nibbling at her bagel, she tried to think about something else, but the only topic that came to mind was one that was just as difficult to make sense of—her feelings for David.

Last night was the best time they had ever had together. David had come over to Jamie while Steve and Shana were locked in their bowling discussion.

"You know, I liked bowling. In high school," he added, sotto voce.

Jamie tried not to giggle. "We can't judge other people's hobbies."

"I guess not. Just like you shouldn't judge people's choices about careers."

"You know, David, I think that's a very wise statement," Jamie said, smiling up at him.

They had danced and laughed and found lots of things that they both liked. It helped, she supposed, that the topic of acting didn't come up all evening. The best part of the evening came when David suggested that they go for a walk.

"A walk? Now?"

"Why not?"

It was a heavenly night. The air was soft and sweet. The nightclub was set high up in the Hollywood Hills, and there was a panoramic view of the city awaiting them outside.

"Are the photographers still around?" Jamie asked nervously.

"They're all in front. We came out the back way."

"We shouldn't stay too long," Jamie warned.

David took her in his arms. "Just long enough for this," he whispered as he kissed her.

Out of a sense of propriety, Jamie went home with Steve, and David had left with Shana. Jamie was sorry now that they all felt the need to be so polite. She was sure that all of them had wished they were leaving with other people.

Jamie hoped that she would hear from David today, but when the telephone rang, and Jamie jumped to get it, Steve was on the other end.

He started without preamble. "Jamie, look, I've got to tell you that I want to start seeing Shana."

"This is not surprising news, Steve."

"It showed?" His laugh was tinged with embarrassment.

"Let's see, when you weren't talking to her, you were dancing with her, and the rest of the time you were getting her food. Yeah, it showed."

"It was like electricity. I know that sounds corny, but belicve me . . ."

"I know, a bolt from the blue. You don't have to rub it in."

"What about you and David?" Steve asked slyly. "You two seemed to be having a pretty good time."

"We were." Jamie wanted Steve to know he wasn't the only who had gotten an electric shock last night.

"So everything's cool, Jamie, right?"

Jamie knew she could make Steve feel bad about the evening if she wanted to, but what was the point? Why shouldn't everyone be happy? "Yeah, it's cool."

"Good." Steve sounded relieved. "Jamie," he continued slowly, "you've been a good friend to me. I hope it will always be that way."

"I can say the same thing."

"I hope it works out for you."

"For all of us," Jamie agreed.

After hanging up, Jamie decided to take a shower and

change her clothes. Maybe David would come over, and for once she wanted to look presentable.

But by 11:30 there had still been no word from David. Jamie was pacing the floor so much that even her mother, unpacking the groceries, noticed. "Don't you have anything better to do on your day off than wear out the floor?"

"I'm not used to time off."

"Take me to the park," Elsie said, tugging at Jamie's sweater.

"Not now, sweetmeat."

"Why? Are you doing something else?"

It was pretty clear, even to a four-year-old, that she wasn't. "All right. But first I have to make a phone call." It was late enough to phone Alison.

Jamie decided to make the call from her bedroom. Her mother didn't know about Alison's incident, and she didn't want to worry her. Hoping that Alison would answer, she dialed her number, but it was Mrs. Blake who picked up.

"Mrs. Blake, is Alison home?"

"Who is this?"

"Jamie."

"Oh." Jamie could hear the relief in Mrs. Blake's voice. "I'm sorry, it's just that I'm screening Alison's calls, and I didn't recognize your voice."

"I heard there was trouble last night."

Mrs. Blake lowered her voice. "I really can't talk about it right now, Jamie."

"But is Alison all right?"

"She's shaken a little, but yes, she's fine. I'll tell her you called."

"Thanks." Jamie wished she could get a few more details, but it was clear Mrs. Blake was anxious to get off the phone. "Tell Alison I'm thinking about her."

"I will."

Maybe a trip to the park would clear her head, Jamie thought as she grabbed a jean jacket. It would be fun to hang out with Elsie, anyway.

Her dad was sitting at the kitchen table drinking a cup of coffee when Jamie went to find Elsie. "Hi, Dad." For a fleeting second, she thought she might like to kiss him on top of the head, but she didn't. *What's with you, Jamie? Going soft?* she asked herself.

Even though she didn't kiss him, Jamie did sit down across the table from him.

"How are you, Dad?"

Her father looked at her searchingly. "How are you?"

"I'm fine."

Mr. O'Leary looked around, obviously making sure that Mrs. O'Leary and Elsie were out of earshot. "I don't think you are, my girl."

Jamie fiddled with a crumpled napkin. "I don't know what you mean."

"Jamie," Mr. O'Leary said in a lowered voice, "will you have lunch with me tomorrow? I'd really like to talk to you."

She was set to say no, that she was busy, but there was such honest concern in her father's eyes that Jamie shook her head. "All right."

"Good." His smile was warming. "I'll call you tomorrow and set it up."

Elsie ran over to them. "The park," she said, pouting a little.

"Yes, yes." Jamie got up and said, "Let's go."

Elsie's favorite part of the park was the swings, so Jamie walked Elsie over to them and sat down on the bench so she could watch Elsie swing away. She was lost in thought when David sat down next to her.

"What are you doing here?" Jamie asked in surprise.

"We met here, don't you remember?" David asked. "But to tell the truth, I stopped at your house, and your dad said you were here."

"I'm glad you came," Jamie smiled. Why pretend now?

"Me, too. I had a really great time last night, Jamie. I hope that isn't a problem for you?"

"A problem? Why?"

"Well, I know you've been seeing Steve."

"Just barely. Besides, didn't you notice Steve and Shana last night? They're an item, big time."

David's face lit up. "That's great. I mean, if it doesn't bother you."

"It doesn't."

David reached over and took her hand, "Jamie, like Humphrey Bogart said in *Casablanca,* I think this is the start of a beautiful friendship."

Chapter 10

Alison found it a little hard to comprehend. Here she was in her living room, talking to a policeman and a detective. The whole scene seemed like a dream. Or maybe a nightmare.

"So you think this person may be someone Alison knows?" Mr. Blake asked Detective Anderson. "Why? There are a million crazy fans out there."

The detective nodded. "But most fans couldn't get into a party at Verdi."

"It could be someone connected with the show," the officer, Patrolman Taylor, suggested.

Faces of her co-workers whirled through Alison's mind. Suddenly, every man she worked with seemed like a potential enemy.

"Do you have any idea who that might be?" Patrolman Taylor asked her.

Alison just shook her head.

Detective Anderson turned to Alison's parents. "A

stalking situation is nothing to be taken lightly, as I'm sure you know.''

''What can we do?'' Mrs. Blake asked worriedly.

''We've had some success with smoking these people out,'' the detective said, ''but that's not without risks.''

''What do you mean, officer?'' Mr. Blake asked.

''I would like Alison to try and make contact with this person.''

''What!'' Alison exclaimed.

Officer Anderson continued quietly. ''The next time this guy calls, get him talking, try to set up a meeting.''

''Too dangerous,'' Mr. Blake said, shaking his head.

''Alison will contact us, and we'll follow her.''

''You're leaving her wide open to danger,'' Mr. Blake reiterated.

''Sir, if we don't take control of this situation, a repeat of Thursday night could happen.''

The discussion went back and forth, assessing the pros and cons of the situation. The police also suggested that the Blakes or the show hire some private investigators as well. The police department couldn't afford to watch Alison around the clock. Finally, Mrs. Blake turned to Alison. ''What do you think, Ali?''

''I want to have this over,'' she said, faltering a little. ''And if the best way to do that is follow the officers' plan, I suppose we'd better do it.''

So the plan was set. Josh Marinello was hired as Alison's bodyguard. She was to wait for the next time the stalker made phone contact, and then Alison would try to set up a meeting. Josh and the police would take it from there. Although the prospect was terrifying, Alison was surprised to find she felt relieved. Maybe, maybe, if things went as planned, this nightmare would be over. But that, Alison knew, was a very big if.

Jamie looked around the restaurant, and saw her father sitting in a corner booth. Smiling at the hostess, who seemed to recognize her, Jamie made her way over to Mr. O'Leary.

"Dad, this doesn't seem like your kind of place," she greeted him.

"Why not?"

"I don't know. Light, airy, lots of hanging plants. It doesn't seem like you."

Jamie was well aware of the fact that she was chattering mindlessly. Her father obviously wasn't just here for a quiche.

"I like pretty things," he said quietly.

"Oh, I didn't mean that. I just associate you with dim lights and leather."

"You mean like bars or taverns?"

"No, Dad."

"I admit I used to hang out in places like that."

Jamie had thought this conversation would be about her weight. Why was her father bringing up the fact that he used to spend some time in bars. She picked up the menu that was lying on the table.

"C'mon, Dad. Let's order."

"Are you actually going to eat what you order?" her father inquired.

So here it was. Even though her problem with food was scaring her, Jamie wasn't sure she could talk about it with her dad. "Of course," she said, trying to sound cheery. "I hear they have good salads here."

Mr. O'Leary gently pushed the menu away from Jamie's face.

"I think you need a little more than a salad. Doctor Wright does too. He called me."

Jamie could feel herself getting angry. "So what would you like me to eat?" She picked up the menu again and began naming dishes. "Stew? That's nice and heavy. What about a roast beef sandwich? I could have it with french fries."

"Jamie, you don't have to be sarcastic. We'll get through this."

That calmed Jamie a little. When the waitress came to take her order, she asked for a bowl of chicken noodle soup. It wasn't much, but at least it was something she could choke down.

Mr. O'Leary reached over to stroke Jamie's hand. Both of them were aware of how thin and bony her fingers were.

"Can you talk to me?" he asked.

Jamie shook her head. "I don't think so." Even though her usually blustery father was being so gentle, she didn't want to talk about her diet.

"Do you mind if I talk?"

Jamie shook her head.

"I'm going to talk about myself a little. I don't know if

you remember, but when I was living with you and your mother, I enjoyed a couple of drinks every night.''

''I remember.''

''When I moved away, I could see where my drinking could become a problem. I had so much time on my hands, you see, and of course, I felt guilty, and the drinking eased that feeling a little. If I hadn't been paying attention, I could have gone off the deep end. But I made sure it didn't become a problem. Now, I only drink once in a while. At a party or special occasion.''

''Why are you telling me this?'' Jamie asked. ''I don't drink at all.''

''Drinking is just one kind of compulsive behavior, Jamie girl. Dieting is another.''

Jamie shakily picked up her spoon. ''I needed to lose some weight. The camera adds ten pounds.'' She wondered how long she had been using that worn line as an excuse.

''You've lost some weight. You can't tell me no one at the studio has noticed how thin you've gotten.''

''Actually, Randy Ellis said something to me about it.''

''There, that should tell you something.''

''Yeah, it tells me that he's going to kick me off the show if I don't put on some weight.'' Jamie's face crumpled. ''But I don't think I can!''

Then it all came spilling out, how she had innocently started the diet and then kept going, far below the weight where she knew she should be. Now, food was disgusting to her, and she didn't want to eat at all.

"I don't think I can control this anymore," Jamie said, tears falling down her cheeks.

"Then we'll get you help," Mr. O'Leary said firmly. "Psychologists, support groups, we'll find you the right ones. Don't worry, darling."

Jamie felt a spark of hope awaken inside her. "Really?"

"Really. Your mother and I will be right beside you every step of the way, and I'm sure your friends will be, too."

Her friends. Jamie realized that for the first time in a long time, she really did have friends. Steve, Mike, Alison, and most of all David. There really was something to get well for.

"I want to do something about this," Jamie said. "I know I have a problem."

Her father nodded approvingly. "Jamie, being able to admit that is the first step toward getting better."

Alison looked nervously around the studio. She searched the faces of the male production members that walked by, and the crew. The only one she trusted completely besides Mike was Josh, who was working undercover as a stage hand. The police had been absolutely insistent that their plan be kept under wraps, but Alison had also insisted on telling Mike, and her parents concurred. She was to downplay the incident at Verdi to everyone else, and the few people on the show who knew, like Randy, had been instructed to do the same.

Randy. She had a message that as soon as she got settled at the set, she was supposed to go and see him.

Jamie and Shana were waiting in her dressing room, and Alison knew they were going to be full of questions. Sure enough, as soon as she came in, Jamie said, "Alison, you never called me back this weekend. Didn't your mother give you the messages?"

"Yeah, she did, Jamie. Thanks."

"So what happened?" Jamie persisted. "I kept leaving messages on Mike's machine, but I didn't hear from him, either."

Alison shrugged. "I got locked in a closet by someone. We thought it might be that crazy fan, but the police think it was just an accident." Alison saw the disbelief on her friends' faces. Maybe she wasn't much of an actress after all.

"So," she continued, turning away, "everything's okay."

"But the letters, the calls . . ." Shana asked, confused.

"We still don't know about them, but the police said it happens all the time to celebrities. So, have you seen the script for this week's show?"

Jamie and Shana looked at each other. It was pretty clear that Alison was making an all-out effort to change the subject. Jamie sensed that there was more here than Alison was ready to talk about, but she also knew that it was important to Alison that they drop it right now.

"The script just arrived," Jamie said, pointing to the coffee table. "One for each of us."

"Mmm, that reminds me, I have to see Randy."

"Randy?" Shana asked.

"He left a message that he wants to see me. Probably about all this stuff," she said lightly.

Without waiting for any more questions, Alison headed toward Randy's office. A tap on the shoulder made her whirl around.

"Oh, it's you," she said catching her breath.

"You've got to try to calm down, Ali," Mike said, steering her off into a corner. "We have no idea how long it's going to take for this guy to surface again. In the meantime, just take it easy, will you? Can you?"

"I don't know," Alison replied honestly.

"I'm right here with you, babe."

"I know," Alison said gratefully. "Between you and Josh, I feel pretty safe. Right now, though, it's first problems first. I've been summoned to Randy's office."

"Then I'm coming with you."

"I don't know . . ."

"I'm coming," he insisted.

"All right."

It was clear from the look on Randy's face, he wasn't expecting both of them. "Malone, I want to talk to Alison."

"You can say anything you want in front of me."

Randy's face twisted into an ugly smile. "I thought I told you two to stay away from each other."

"I can have friends, can't I?" Alison said boldly.

"Fine. If that's the way you want to play it. We'll deal

with that later. Right now, I want to talk about this so-called stalker that's after you.''

"So-called?" Mike asked, outraged.

"Calm down," Randy said. "And sit down. Now, the police have filled me in on this plan. I hope it's not going to disrupt the set or get into the newspapers."

"Why would we want to tell anyone?" Alison asked.

"Maybe this is all a publicity stunt."

Mike got up. "We don't have to listen to this."

"You do as long as I'm in charge. Now, I'm willing to cooperate with the police, but I've got a show to put on. Alison, I want you, and I suppose you, too, Mike, to do what you've been hired to do around here."

"You are some piece of work, Randy," Mike said, pulling Alison to her feet. "Don't worry. We know the show must go on. No matter who's in danger."

Chapter 11

Mike may have promised Randy the show would go on, but Alison wasn't sure she was giving much of a performance, onstage or off.

She knew that Jamie, Shana, and some of the others suspected there had been trouble, but everyone was keeping quiet about it. Good thing, too, because Alison thought if anyone even mentioned the word *stalker,* she might scream.

Onstage, she could barely concentrate and was afraid that pretty soon Randy might have good cause to get rid of her. There had been one more letter, a rambling piece that apologized for putting her in the closet, but the writer said he had gotten scared when he heard someone coming. He wanted her to know that he wasn't a violent guy, he only wanted to make her happy, and that someday he would prove that to her. Alison had turned the letter over to the police. But there hadn't been any more phone calls, so Alison hadn't been able to put their plan into effect. She couldn't be seen talking to Josh on the set. He was more a comforting presence in the background than an immediate help.

As the week wore on, Alison knew that she was going to have to get herself focused on something else. Otherwise she would totally lose it. Then it hit her. Sure, she had her own problems, but there were other people hurting on this show, too. She had promised herself she was going to talk to Jamie about her dieting. *Get your mind off yourself, Alison. Jamie needs you.*

But Alison wasn't sure how to broach the topic. Invite Jamie out to lunch? That seemed a little cruel. There was a nice tree-shaded park at the back of the studio. Maybe she and Jamie could just sit out there at lunchtime and talk things over.

Jamie was delighted with the invitation. She hoped that maybe Alison was ready to take her into her confidence about the stalker.

It was a gorgeous day, not too hot, and Alison and Jamie settled themselves on one of the picnic benches under a leafy palm tree.

Alison watched the men who walked by, studying their faces.

"Do you think it could be one of them?" Jamie asked quietly.

"What?" Alison's head snapped around.

"The guy who writes the letters."

Alison tried to shrug off the topic. "Who knows?"

"There's that guy who works in the cafeteria. He's a little strange," Jamie said. "And what about that carpenter, Karl. He's always hanging around the cast."

"Jamie, I don't want to talk about this."

"You don't?" Jamie asked with surprise. "I thought that's why you brought me out here."

"No. No, I want to talk about you."

"Me?"

"Jamie, we started this conversation once before, and we got interrupted."

Jamie looked away. "I get it. This is about my dieting."

"I know this is rough . . ."

"No," Jamie said, turning back, "I can talk about it, now. Because I finally woke up to the fact I have to do something about it."

"Jamie, that's great," Alison said with relief. "For a while there, I didn't think you knew what was happening."

"For a while, I didn't." Jamie played with her braid. "At least, I couldn't admit it."

"What changed?" Alison asked.

"A lot of things. I knew I was out of control. I wanted to be well because of David. And then I had a talk with my father."

"Your father? I thought you two hardly got along."

Jamie was quiet for a moment. "What can I say? When I needed him, he came through for me."

"That's great, Jamie," Alison said sincerely. "Fathers can do that sometimes."

She thought about her own father. Even though Mr. Blake had tried to hide it, because he didn't want to add to her misery, it was clear he was upset, not only because of the circumstances, but because she hadn't let him in on what was happening at the studio.

Tiptoeing around the topic was painful for both of them, so Alison was relieved when he had taken her out for a ride last Sunday and they had cleared the air.

She tried to explain. "There were a lot of reasons I didn't want to tell you, Dad. I was tired of being your Alison Wonderland, and like I told you, I was afraid you'd make me quit the show."

"Don't forget Mike. You were pretty mad at me about Mike, weren't you?"

Alison nodded.

Mr. Blake cleared his throat. "I know I'm not the freest man with my feelings, Ali, but if anything happened to you . . ." The frog in his throat became a choke.

"Daddy, nothing's going to happen to me."

Her father straightened up. "It certainly isn't." He put his arm around Alison and pulled her close to him. "We'll find a happy medium, Ali. I promise not treat you like a china doll anymore. As soon as we catch this nut case, anyway. 'Til then, you're stuck with me."

Jamie broke into her thoughts. "You know, I envied you your dad."

"I'm lucky," Alison agreed. "We both are."

"Alison, you've got to concentrate," Mike said after rehearsal on Thursday. "You've got to be ready to tape tomorrow."

"I'll be all right. What does Donna always say? When the cameras go on, you start flying on automatic pilot."

"Say, how about we go down to Malibu and relax for a while?"

Alison smiled wanly. "I think I'd better go home and take a nap. Besides, you know Josh would be right behind us."

Mike smiled. "Just what we need, a six-foot-two chaperon."

"You can give me a ride home, though," Alison said, "I just have to check in with Josh. He can follow behind us."

She was about to find Josh, when the burly investigator found her. "You have a call, Alison," he told her.

Before this mess had started, Alison rarely got calls. "Do you think it's him?" she whispered.

"Let's find out."

Heading for the phone, the phone that the police had tapped, Alison tried to remember everything she was supposed to do. Sound pleasant, encourage the guy to meet her. Was she that good an actress? Josh was right behind her as she picked up the phone in a private office.

"Hello?"

Silence.

"I know you're there," she said, trying to sound upbeat.

"Alison?"

"Yes. Who is this?"

There was more silence.

"Look, you don't have to meet me in hallways. Why don't we just get together and talk?"

"You don't want to talk to me," a deep voice with a slight accent replied.

"Why not?" Alison scrambled to think of something else to say. "I like to get to know my fans."

"You're sweet, you know."

"Thanks." She glanced at her watch. The police had told her it took at least three minutes to trace a call, but she wasn't even close yet. "So can we get together?"

More silence, then, "You know that Pie House in the Valley?"

Alison didn't know the San Fernando Valley at all, and certainly not a place called the Pie House, but she assured him she did.

"I know you can't feel too safe with me yet, so take one of the limos I've seen you in."

"The limo? That would be good."

Alison remembered to ask what he'd be wearing.

"A blue-and-white checked shirt." With that, he hung up.

"You couldn't trace it, could you?" Alison asked Josh when the line went dead.

"Nope. But I'll call the police for backup. And we'll be right behind you."

"Oh, thank goodness," Alison said with relief.

Mike walked into the office looking for Alison and immediately figured out what was going on. "He called."

Alison and Josh filled him in.

"Can't you drive the limo?" Mike asked Josh.

"I thought about that, but someone might be watching. It's better to pretend this is just a normal trip."

"Then I want to ride with you, Josh."

"First I have to call the police," said Josh. "We'll need some to come with us and others to meet us there."

"Now we want this to look totally normal," Josh said a few minutes later as he walked a pale Alison down the hall. "Just in case this guy is around and watching."

"Tell me about him," Mike said.

"He had an accent, European, I think, and said he was going to be wearing a blue-and-white checked shirt."

Mike frowned.

"What?" Alison demanded.

"I'm not sure. There's something . . ."

At the door they could see Alison's usual black limo parked across the lot in its spot. "We don't want anyone to see you being accompanied into the limo," Josh said, "so we'll wait here and you'll walk the rest of the way yourself. Officer Taylor's car is right in front here and we'll be right behind you."

Alison wanted to kiss Mike, but knew someone might be watching even now. Taking a deep breath, she headed for the limo while Mike watched her go. Her knees were so weak, she thought they were going to buckle, and it was only through force of will that she was able to make herself approach the car.

Just as she was opening the door, Mike suddenly shouted, "No!" His voice reverberated throughout the garage.

As Josh watched in amazement, Mike ran over to the

car, and pushed Alison away from the door. Then he pulled the frightened driver out of the car. "Come here, Josh."

Josh ran up to them. "What's going on?"

"This is Karl, one of the carpenters," Mike told Josh. "But he's just begun doubling sometimes as a limo driver. Jamie and I had him the night of the party."

"What's this all about?" Karl asked nervously.

Alison's eyes widened. "The accent. I never noticed it before."

Mike pulled open the jacket Karl was wearing. Underneath was a blue-and-white checked shirt.

The police arrived and Josh told them he thought they'd caught their stalker.

Officer Taylor nodded to some of his men, "Get this guy out of here. We'll question him down at the station." Josh turned to Mike, "Pretty good detective work, Malone. How did you know?"

"It just all came together. I've been watching Karl for a while, but I didn't realize he drove the limo, too. That must be how he got into the party. When Ali told me about the accent and the shirt, it all clicked." He turned and took Alison in his arms. "Are you all right?"

She leaned her head against his chest and nodded. "I am now."

For the first time in a long time, Alison and Jamie agreed that they were finally utterly relaxed. "And if you want to relax," Jamie said, "your backyard is a great place to do it, Ali."

Alison nodded, her eyes closed. "How long can you stay?"

"I have an appointment with my therapist later this afternoon."

"You like her, right?"

"Yeah I do. I put on a pound this week," Jamie said quietly.

Alison opened her eyes. "Great," she smiled.

"I know I'm in this for the long haul, but I feel like I'm going in the right direction for a change."

"Hey, guys." There was Mike coming down the walk.

"I didn't expect you until tonight," Alison said, shading her eyes.

"I've got big news!" His smile was so big, it seemed to have taken over his face. "Randy is history!"

"He got fired?" Jamie asked excitedly.

"Seems the network brass woke up. They weren't any happier with the way he was running the show than we were."

"Is Dan coming back?" Alison wanted to know.

"Scuttlebutt has it that Kate's going to take his job. But who cares? Randy's gone, and we've got our show back. This is the best!"

Alison and Jamie smiled at each other. Mike was more right than he knew. This really was the best.